The Mafia Identity

Nerd Turn Mafia Lord

Goodness Loveday

Henry Loveday

ISBN-9798842761708

Cover design by: Art Painter
Library of Congress Control Number: 2018675309
Printed in the United States of America

CONTENTS

INTRODUCTION

Sometimes what seems to be reality may actually just be an illusion, a facade far from reality. Sometimes who we are, what we do, and how we live may turn out to be just a front and we may not even know.

Russel Pennington is the only son and child of the Pennington couple. Having been home-schooled his whole life and barely have any contact with the outside except through novels and stories from his parents.

He was the male version of princess Repunzel from the Disney movie Tangled. Only he didn't live in a tower and this wasn't a fairytale

Wanting to experience life like a normal teenager, he requested to attend a high school instead of being home-schooled.

His wish was granted, though it didn't go as simply as he had expected.

Such a simple request unraveled a huge secret that would change his life forever.

How life-changing could the secret change the life of this quirky nerd?

Well, read to find out in, Mafia Identity.

(SUBTITLE: A Nerd Turn Mafia Lord)

Genres

Characters:

Male lead............Russel Pennington

Female lead.............Irma Agalos

Side characters:..........Larry and Sabrina Pennington as Russel's parents ......Mr. Agalos

Other Characters will be added as the story goes on...

CHAPTER 1: FINALLY, I'LL GO TO HIGH SCHOOL

Russell Pennington:

"And that's how to use Newton's force theory" I mumbled scribbling on my notebook.

I heaved a sigh when I was done, physics sure is a hard subject. I picked a novel out of my bedside shelf. "A TALE OF TWO CITIES, by Charles Dickens. "Wow, this would be interesting, I opened the next page and began reading, page after page, I read in my room.

"Russell, Russell," my mom called, but I was too engrossed in the book to hear her.

France, less favored on the whole as to matters spiritual than her sister of the shield and trident, rolled with exceeding smoothness downhill. Making paper money and spending it. Under the guidance of her Christian pastors,….. Mom enters…..

"R.U.S.S.E.L" my mom yelled barging into my room. I yelped falling off the bed, my glasses fell off my face. My vision became blurry as I raised my head to stare at my mom. I heard her walk up to me, and I wore my glasses back on my nose. I adjusted it and my vision became clear.

"Hey mom, you're back" I sat up.

"Yeah, we got hell-stressed out today at the market," she said, taking off her face mask and scarf.

She was dressed in a kind of cat burglar outfit.

"Mom, can I ask you a question," I asked.

"What is it dear " she ruffled my hair.

"Why do you and dad use disguises when going out, and why can't I follow you guys," I asked.

"Russ, you've asked those questions a million times, and I've answered you. The world is dangerous! We can't go out without these disguises or else we'll be harmed...... And we don't want you to get hurt." she said.

"But, I've been inside this house for too long, won't I go to high school like my peers... .....won't I get a job and get married, what's so bad about the world that you're so scared of," I asked all at once.

"Just come down for dinner Russ," she said, then left the room without answering my questions.

I sighed, picked up my novel, and went to my room balcony. If only I could go out to see the world …. I wish to go to school.

I've been homeschooled my whole life and I'm getting tired of it. Though I am an introvert and shy around people, that's only because I don't go out at all.

I don't mingle with people of my age. Maybe, one day, I'll get to see the outside world.

I stared over the valley, till it was time for dinner.

Mr. Agalos's residence:

"Have you found them yet?" Mr. Agalos asked, crossing his legs on the couch in the living room.

"No boss we haven't found them" his guard replied, head bowed.

Mr. Agalos's face became stiff with anger. For some years now, he's been searching for them. He hired the best men from the most powerful mafias, yet he couldn't find just a man and woman. He puffed his cigarette.

"As soon as you find them, make sure they don't escape, " He said.

"Yes, boss" his guard replied.

At that moment, the two guards positioned at the door opened the door, and Irma Agalos stepped into the living room.

Her hair was in different shades of color, tied up in a doggy style, baggy shirts, and oversize pants, not to talk of the men's drawers she wore.

She had a cigarette in between her lips and she sagged into the house.

"Irma!

What on earth has come over you," Mr. Agalos exclaimed shocked at how his foster daughter looked.

"Hey, old man, sup," Irma puffed out smoke from her nose."

"Oh, my goodness, when did you learn to smoke Irma!" Mr. Agalos almost yelled.

"I learned from the best, enjoy your joint dad," Irma said as she bounced up the stairs. Mr. Agalos stared after her.

Well, he doesn't blame her, she had seen him smoke most time, so she probably began smoking too. But her dressing is still a mystery to him.

"Light me another joint," Mr. Agalos ordered.

His guard put a rolled joint in between his lips and lighted it for him.

Mr. Agalos smoked the joint nodding his head as it made him high.

So Russ, your dad and I have a surprise for you," mom suddenly said as we ate dinner

"What is it?" I asked less bothered about the surprise.

It's maybe just a new novel, spectacles, or clothes. That's the usual surprise I get from my parents.

"You don't sound too happy about our new surprise this time," dad said, cutting into his steak.

"Your mom and I have decided to grant you one of your biggest wishes," dad said gaining my attention.

"Really? tell me," I urged eagerly.

"Oh, look at him, all giddy-up" mom chuckled.

"C'mon you're both killing me with suspense " I whined.

"Alright fine, we've enrolled you in a high school. ...you wished to go to school with your peers right? Now here's the chance, " mom said.

Hold on... mom didn't just say they had me enrolled in a school right?

"Are you serious, you're not joking right?" I asked trying to contain my excitement

"You'll resume on Monday," dad said.

"Yes ...thank you so much...Yippee I'm going to school!"

I squealed rushing to my room.

"Hey Russell, where are you going... you aren't done with your food yet " mom called.

"I'm okay mom," I yelled.

Yes!!. finally, I'll go to high school, I'll get to experience the life of a real student just like I've read in novels.

I can't wait for Monday.

You sure you'll be able to face the bullies....you're a geek ass nerd, my subconscious kicked in.

Oh right, I forgot I'm a nerd and I haven't been to the outside world.

What if I act badly?

What if I'm awkward and stupid?

What if I stutter?

What if I get bullied and can't fight back?

I thought…This will really be a big new change for me, but I hope I can get through it.

First day at school:

"We're here baby, your new school," Mom said, the minute dad pulled up in the schoolyard.

I stared out the window, at the students, most of them were in groups and they chatted with themselves. Everyone seemed to have a partner of their own, and I didn't see anyone wearing geeky glasses like me. Conniption and nervousness gripped me. How will I survive in this kinda school? I began having second thoughts about attending a real school.

"Hey, baby you look stiff…don't you like the school," Mom asked from the front seat.

"No, I like the school. I just don't know if I'll be able to fit in with them," I said lowly.

"Don't worry baby, I'm sure you're gonna ace it….just stay out of trouble, don't make too many friends, and try to stay more in your circle, okay?" Mom rubbed and pulled my cheeks.

"Mmmmhmmm" I nodded.

"Aren't you both coming with me?" I asked, wearing my bag on my back.

"No son, we've got to go, but we've already settled everything with the principal….. And you have your map and timetable so you should be able to get to your class," dad said.

I sighed. Guess I'm alone here.

"Okay, I'll get to class," I adjusted my glasses and got down.

"Bye-bye baby sees ya later" mom waved.

I smiled lightly.

Okay Russ you can do this just act normal, I mentally pumped myself.

"Here we go" I walked past the yard passing some students. I saw a few points and laugh at me, and it kinda made me want to change my mind. ***No I can't give up now*** I walked into the hallway, lockers aligned the walls.

I brought out the map and began looking for my locker. "Oi what is stupid and has four eyes," someone asked loudly as I walked past them." I don't know what," his partner asked. "A Nerd," they burst out laughing and a few others joined them.

I bowed my head and hastened my steps.

"Watch it nerd" someone pushed me forward and I almost fell.

"Sorry" I mumbled.

"Yeah, sorry for yourself hah" the person yelled.

"Get out of here, leave the boy alone," someone else hovered over me, hiding me from the mean guy.

The mean guy scowled and walked away after giving me a mean stare.

The guy who saved me turned and I got a clear view of his face.

"Hey, you alright," he asked

"Yes thank you," I said.

"It's nothing but you better watch for that guy he's a big bully…" the guy said.

"Yeah I'll make sure to do that" I replied.

"I'm Shaun, you" he introduced himself.

"I'm Russell Pennington," I said and we shook hands.

"Nice meeting you Russell, you're new right?" He asked.

I nodded.

"Me too, what year are you," he asked.

"Um.. the second year" I replied.

"Me too, let's find our lockers and class together," he said.

I smiled appreciatively at him.

Well at least not everyone is all bad We walked together and talked about a lot of topics. He was more talkative, and I only ta ed when necessary.

We both found our lockers and surprisingly our lockers were beside each other. I checked my timetable and I had physics class the same as Shaun. He told me so much about the school and who to avoid and who to socialize with. I nodded feebly to every warning he told me. He wasn't a nerd like me but he was nicer than the other students.

"I really wish to join the school's basketball team," Shaun said.

"Yeah you've got a pretty good height," I commented, eyeing his height.

He was about a foot taller than me and I had to stare up at him.

"I would have if not for Nikko," he muttered.

"Who's Nikko," I asked.

"He's the school basketball team leader and the boyfriend of… "loud murmuring sounds came from a crowd behind us.

We turned to find out what the commotion was all about.

Two girls walked in with a boy in between them, the boy held a girl by her hair and was pulling her along.

"The Triple Threatz, " I heard Shaun say.

The boy held the girl's hair and she cried pleading for him to let her go.

"Triple Threatz? " I repeated. "Uh-huh…they're the biggest bullies in this school, Shaun said.

"Who are they," I asked.

Irma Agalos…Tania Hopkin ….Melaina Bithell….. they're the daughters of wealthy and dangerous men, so nobody can stand up to them most especially Irma" Shaun explained. "Really, but you mentioned three girls' names but I saw two girls and a boy," I said confused.

"That's Irma you're referring to as a boy, she's really crazy and mean, she's also a tomboy," Shaun said.

I nodded in understanding.

The Irma pulled the girl's hair harder.

"Please I'm sorry I didn't know you would park there, the space was empty when I parked my car" the girl cried."

"You're lucky I'm in a good mood, scram" Irma yelled letting the girl go.

The girl ran away in tears.

I felt pity, wow so this is what it is like to get bullied.

Triple Threatz passed us and I hid my face from them, I don't ever want to become one of their victims.

"Hey, let's go or we'll be late for class " Shaun urged, as we left for class afterward.

"Hell...Hello, ev..everyone... mm..my name is Russell," I introduced myself to the class when the teacher told me to...

"Sounds like four eyes would be a better name for you Nerd" a girl sneered and the class laughed.

I bent my head in embarrassment.

"That was a mean thing to say, Lennie.

Russell, go and sit there," the teacher said.

I walked up to sit and sat down.

The teacher resumed her lesson and I brought out my book to take notes. Suddenly Irma barged into the glass popping gum loudly.

"Irma you're late again," the teacher sighed.

"Whatever," Irma paid no attention to her.

She began walking to where I sat.

I immediately hid my face in my book, praying she would walk past me.

Soon I perceived a choking perfume.

"Hey, you get off that chair" I heard her yell.

I put the book down from my face.

"Me?" I asked dumbly.

"Yes, you now" she yelled louder.

I hastily took my bag and book and stood to trim the chair.

She pushed me away and sat on the chair crossing her legs on the table.

where would I sit now.

I saw Shaun beckoning me to come to sit beside him.

I did, and the class continued…

CHAPTER 2: YOU'RE ALREADY IN BIG TROUBLE

"Okay that's all today, make sure to do your homework," the teacher said after the electric bell rang.

The other students trooped out in groups, including Irma.

Man!!, That girl sure gives me the creeps

"Hey, c'mon Russell let's go have lunch," Shaun stood up and I followed him out of the class.

"So you were telling about Nikko before Triple Threatz interrupted us" I started up a conversation as we walked the hallway to the cafeteria.

"Yeah, Nickko Ramberg, so-called boyfriend of Irma and the school's basketball team leader......

In my first year, I requested to join the team, but the buffoon made a joke of me and embarrassed me...........

Urge, I wished I was wiser then, I would have given him a good punch and kick to his stupid face.....

After that day he tried to pick on me and so did the other students, but I encouraged myself and I stood for myself....... I didn't let them get the best of me" Shaun said.

"He sounds like a bad guy" I commented.

"He's worse than bad, even worse is better than him...

He thinks because Irma lets him fool around her and make everyone think he is her boyfriend that people would bow at his feet." Shaun scoffed.

"Huh? He isn't Lima's boyfriend " my brows creased.

"Nop" he popped the 'P' sound.

"Nickko spread a rumor about him dating Irma and since Irma didn't deny it everyone took it as though they were dating" Shaun added.

"How are you so sure they aren't dating...for all we know they could be," I said.

"Puh-lease Irma Agalos is a tough nut case to crack....she's the daughter of a mafia lord and no guy has gotten anywhere with her.....

She literally beat up a guy because he asked her out, Nickko is only using her to gain more popularity, power, and free will.......

And I guess Irma is letting him fool himself" Shaun said.

I dropped the topic since we already got to the cafeteria.

Hmmm, the cafeteria wasn't bad at all, pretty nice for teens.

We lined up at the counter waiting for our turn to be served.

There were about 5 peeps before us, so we waited for our turn.

"I have to use the bathroom, Russel, save me this spot," Shaun said, disappearing out of the cafeteria before I could say anything.

Oh no!!

Why did he leave me alone here with all these scary students?

I felt secure with Shaun beside but now he's gone, I felt like a drenched puppy who has been abandoned in a dog park.

And the other dogs were big and scary.

Okay, I know I'm a bit over dramatic but what do expect from someone who hasn't been in the open for like 18 years?

"Move outta the way" I heard a yell behind me which sent fear through me. I turned to see Triple Threatz, and Irma was the one who yelled at me. I bowed my head and made way for them to move to the front of the line. They brushed past me and stood in front of me.

Irma was getting served, Tania stood behind her, and Meliana stood behind Tania. So technically I was behind Meliana.

All three of them were choking and I coughed lightly moving backward bumping into the person behind me.

"Hey watch it" the person snapped pushing me forward.

I lost balance on my feet and I stumbled forward bumping into Melania's back and she, in turn, fell on Tania.

I was quite quick enough to compose myself else I would have fallen on them. The hairs on my skin stood out as goosebumps filled my body.

"Ahhh, are you blind" Tania yelled trying to untangle her legs from Meliana's.

I don't think they noticed I was the cause of the fall so I made to escape from there.

"Hey you, get back here" I felt a grip on the collar of my shirt, and I was turned to face Meliana. Before I could say anything, a slap landed on my face. And my glasses cracked from the impact of the slap "Are you stupid? ....how dare you push me" she yelled.

The attention of the other student rested on us

"I'm sorry, I didn't mean to.." I said, slowly, as she interjected…"Of course, you didn't mean to…those stupid goggles made you blind" she rasped.

"I can't believe this, my outfit is messed up and I'll have to change.

You, you won't get away with this nerd" with that she left the cafeteria.

I gulped.

What did she mean by I won't get away with this?

What did I do wrong? I only bumped into her cause I got pushed

I left there embarrassed. …but I didn't fail to notice the pitiful eyes the others were giving me.

Where is Shaun anyway?

I saw him at the end of the hallway, I waved him over.

"Hey, what happened to you, your face is red and your glass is cracked, " Shaun asked when he got me.

"I got in trouble with Triple Threatz " I replied.

"What did you do," he asked

"Someone pushed me and I bumped into Melania and she fell on Tania

…….so she got mad and slapped me, she also threatened that I won't get away with it" I explained

"Oh my gosh, Russel I only left you for some minutes and you're already in big trouble " Shaun exclaimed

"Big trouble?" I questioned.

"If It had been Irma you bumped into then you would have gotten mercy but you bumped into two devils……

Tania and Melania are the real devils in this school, they make sure whoever annoys them gets punished in unimaginable ways" Shaun said.

More fear grew in me.

"What's gonna happen to me?" I asked scared.

"At the very most, you'll probably become their school slave till they decide to sell you" "Huh" my brows creased.

"Just pray they sell you, getting sold is much better than being their slave," Shaun said.

I didn't have time to process what he said when two huge guys appeared out of nowhere and grabbed me.

"Hey, what are you doing? ..let me go" I yelled trying to get out of their grip as they pulled me with them.

Shaun had a look of helplessness and at that moment I knew I was done for.

CHAPTER 3: BRIEF INTRODUCTION OF TRIPLE THREATZ

Lrma Agalos, 18 and eleven months old, is a foster daughter of mafia Lord, Agalos. Mr. Agalos owned the mafia surrounding Mazatlan USA and Mexico City. And, the importing of cocaine, marijuana etcetera, through the underground borders of Mexico and Mazatlan. Agalos adopted Irma from an orphanage 11 years ago and he had single-handedly raised her in the mafia lifestyle.

Irma is a sniper, she sometimes helps Agalos inspect the import of the drugs and make accounts. She also does the killing of men who tried to cheat Agalos. Two things Irma lacked were a fun life and a mother's care so she turned into a tomboy.

Tania Hopkin, the second of three children of the Hopkins family, she's really sassy, and mean. She's overly obsessed with being perfect and pretty.

Typical spoilt brat Meliana Bithell, the only daughter and last child of the Bithell family. There wasn't much of a difference between Melania and Tania. As they were both spoiled brats, sassies, and meanies, and thought too highly of themselves. She and Tania made a habit of making their offenders their school slaves till they then exchange slaves. Sometimes they sell off their school slaves to other meanies in school and most of their victims were nerds like Russel.

The school authorities can't do anything about whatever the girls do, because the girl's fathers were well-known dangerous men and they wouldn't want to get into a bad book with them.

I tried squirming out of the guy's hands but they held me tighter

"Quite down kid" one said.

His scary voice made me whimper in fear.

I wondered who they were and where they were taking me to.

I cursed myself for not being contented with my homeschooling.

If I had been contented with that then I wouldn't be getting bullied like this, or get in trouble with some mean girls, or get dragged by scary-looking men.

I wished I could turn back the hands of time and I would take back my wish to school in a real high school.

Too late now, I just had to accept whatever comes to my way.

I watched dumbly as my legs dragged onto the floor as I was held by my arms. I couldn't see clearly with my cracked glasses so it was hard to tell where I was taken to. I heard a door open and then close and the men let go of my arms.

I fell to the floor.

"Great you've brought the clumsy" a girl said, I looked up trying to make out who she was with my blurry vision.

Inside Triple Threatz private classrooms:)

Melania's guards left the room leaving Russel behind.

"Where am I " Russel was appalled and his blurry vision wasn't helping matters Meliana ignored him and turned to Tania, and asked: "What do you think we should do to him" "The usual, he'll be our school slave " Tania shrugged.

Irma was in a corner, eyes closed and headphones plugged in her ear. She wasn't listening to music, she was listening to Meliana and Tania's conversation, though, she wasn't interested in whatever they'll do to their victim.

"Nah…I want to do something different this time….why don't we sell him to Nickko."

At the mention of Nickko, Russell's breath hitched.

He had guessed he was in the same room with Triple Threatz and they were probably talking about what to do with him.

"Yeah, Nickko did mention his team needed a water boy," Tania said.

"Please, I'm sorry I didn't mean to bump into you…I got pushed please forgive me " Russel pleaded.

"Shut up nerd" Meliana yelled.

Hearing a boy's voice, Irma opened her eyes and saw Russel in a kneeling position. She at once recognized him as the new nerd boy. She scoffed at how frail and weak he looked. ***He wouldn't last long under Nickko, and he might get raped by him,***Irma thought. Irma knew Nickko was a bisexual and he took pleasure in abusing weak boys and nerds. She took a good look at Russel, she shook her head in pity.

"Poor boy, first day in school and he's in trouble," Irma said in pity.

"Hey, Irma, could you ask Nickko if he still needs a water boy for his team, " Meliana asked.

"Mmmm" Irma cleared her throat and stood up from her corner

"I need a new slave would you mind selling him to me," Irma asked.

"Ooh, well you know how it is Irma, you'll pay a huge cash for him" Meliana chuckled "How much do you want" Irma rolled her eyes.

"$10,000 isn't a big amount right" Meliana licked her lips.

"What, that's a huge amount for just a nerdy weak boy" Irma was shocked at the amount Meliana mentioned.

Russel felt ashamed that the girls were pricing over him.

"C'mon Irma it's not like the money is a huge amount to you... your dad is a drug lord so I'm sure you've enough money to spare if you need a school slave" Meliana twirled her hair around her finger.

Irma turned to look at Russel, he was squinting his eyes to see them.

$10,000 wasn't a huge amount to her anyway, but will she spend it on a vulnerable boy?

CHAPTER 4: YOU ARE MY SCHOOL SLAVE

Immersed in thoughts Irma turned to stare at the nerd again. She checked him out. Geeky, wuss, douche, dorky, those seemed a little too much but that was the perfect description of the nerd. Meliana patiently waited for Irma to make her decision, she always hoped for situations like this so she could leech Irma. Irma was way wealthier than her so she could get a few bucks from her.

"If the money is too much for you to pay, I won't mind selling him to Nickko" Meliana shrugged hoping Irma would agree to her amount.

"I'll buy him " pausing for a while Irma continued…. "but I offer you $9,000."

"Great he's all yours " Meliana giggled.

She thought of the new designer bag she saw at the mall the other day. Now she would have enough money to buy it.

"I'll send the money to you" turning to the nerd Irma ordered: "Hey nerd, get your ass up and follow me."

"Uh…I…I can't see" Russel stuttered.

Confused, Irma inquired "you can't see?"

"Yeah…my glasses are broken" Russel added "I can't see without it."

"Seriously…how will you walk around without it" Irma snapped.

"I have extra glasses in my locker, I just need to get them " Russel answered.

Irma sighed, she didn't know why she wanted this nerd to be her school slave but whatever it is she'll find out later.

"Get up and start walking, I'll lead you to your locker" she pursed her lips.

Russel hesitated for a while before getting up.

"Turn around and start walking," Irma ordered.

Russel did as told, and she began leading him from behind, though she did yell at him a few times.

They got to Russel's locker and he opened it scouring for his bag, he got it, took out another pair of glasses, and wore it.

His sight cleared off, "Thank you."

"Whatever, now I'm sure you know who I am and what I am. You are my school slave as I have paid a huge price to save your wuss ass...."

Without waiting for his reply Irma continued: "From now on you'll do everything I tell you. You'll hold my bag and books, do my homework, get my food. And also, you must be early before me and basically follow me everywhere in school..... And, let me make this clear to you nerd, don't push my buttons or delay me, I promise you won't like it."

Gulping scared to death, Russell's entire body became sweaty including his ass. He only wanted to attend school and not serve as someone's school slave.

"You get me, nerd," Irma inquired.

Russell vigorously nodded not wanting to annoy her.

"Good, it's time for homeroom, the day would soon be over, your work as my school slave starts tomorrow......see you tomorrow school slave" Irma gave him a sinister smile which almost made

Russel pee his pants.

She walked off sagging.

Russel heaved a huge sigh of relief once she was out of sight, this isn't what he wanted but he had no choice.

He didn't want to be hurt more than he already was.

"Guess I better head for home" Russel took his bag, shut his locker, and left for class. End of the day.

"You're a lucky man..,. Irma made you her school slave, you won't be bullied anymore, you'll get special treatment,… only that you have to do everything she says… .even if she says you should wipe her ass." Russel wasn't listening to Shaun's rambling about how lucky he is to be Irma's school slave.

But the last line irked him.

"Wipe her ass?" He arched his brow.

"Nah I'm just kidding, you should see the look on your face" Shaun chuckled.

Without waiting for his reply Shaun inquired, "Will you take the train home, or do you have someone coming over to pick you up?"

"My parents would come for me" Russel replied.

"Okay bud, I gotta catch the train now see you tomorrow" Shaun waved walking away.

Russel waved back and then began his wait for his parents when his eyes caught sight of Irma with a guy.

"Can I kiss you, babe?" Nickko pouted his lips at Irma.

"Let those things come near me and I'll bite them off" Irma warned disgusted by his act.

"C'mon babe we are in a relationship so we have to kiss, make…..
heyyy, where are you going," Nickko asked angrily.

Irma walked off ignoring his speech.

"Bitch" Nickko cursed, watching Lrma walk away.

CHAPTER 5: LEAVE HIM ALONE

The next day, Lrma walked into the school with her usual steps, Tania and Meliana were on each side of her. As they walked the other students paved the way for them, and some scurried away. Nickko met up with them with his basketball buddies.

"Hey, babe " Niccko attempted to kiss Irma but she turned her face and he kissed her cheeks instead.

Frowning at his failed attempt to kiss her he whispered " c'mon Irma don't humiliate me like this in front of everyone…let me kiss you."

Seeing his lips pouted and itching to her face, Irma walked off leaving him to sort himself.

Red with embarrassment and anger, Nickko yelled at the students who dared to lurk around the area.

They immediately scurried off murmuring.

Stupid bitch he cursed fuming.

Meliana stared at him mockingly, "better luck next time," she said walking away.

Tania patted Nikko's chest, slipping a folded paper into his breast pocket. She then winked cat walked away.

Nickko smirked knowing what she did, dipping his hands into his breast pocket he took out the paper.

Changing Room, School's Gymnasium:

"Bitch seems hungry for me today " he murmured to himself.

Keeping the paperback, he headed for homeroom, and his buddies followed behind him.

Russel sighed as he got to homeroom, he had successfully evaded Irma and he hoped to continue that way for the rest of the day.

He prayed she wouldn't have a homeroom so as not to see her.

No one was in class so he took a seat, placed his head on the desk, and waited for everyone to arrive.

Minutes later the loud chattering of other students was heard as they settled down. Deciding not to lift his head till he hears a teacher's voice, Russel kept his head down.

Wham!!!! A heavy bag landed on his head, his hands immediately went to his head as he winced looking up.

There stood Irma with an angry expression.

"What did I tell you about holding my bag for me" she inquired yelling attracting the attention of other students.

"…..I…I…I'm sorry I forgot" he apologized gulping.

"This better be the last time this would happen" Irma huffed and took her seat.

Russel then picked up her bag and held it still wincing from the impact of the bag. He wondered what she had in the bag that made it so heavy.

Soon enough, a teacher came in and then began teaching. Russel well to pass Irma the books and stationaries she needed during the class.

And after a few classes, it was lunch break and Russel accompanied Irma to the cafeteria holding her bag.

Walking towards the Triple Threatz special booth, Tania and

Meliana were seated there waiting for her.

"Hey, there, nerdy slave boy," Meliana taunted.

Russel pursed his lips bowing his head.

Ignoring the scene Irma took a seat and brought out some bucks from her wallet.

Handing it to Russel, she said to him: "I want 2 scones and a club sandwich."

Pausing for a while she added, "make sure to add some and a smoothie."

Remembering getting Irma's food was part of his slave job. So Russel took the money and went to get it.

Nickko got to the cafeteria and walked toward the Triple Threatz booth. Seeing him Tania winked smiling sheepishly.

Nickko then returned the act, "You wanna eat without me? That's not fair to your boyfriend" Nickko scrunched his eyebrows at Irma.

She ignored him and plugged in her earphones.

Cussing, Nickko turned his attention to the other two.

Russel returned to the booth with Irma's orders and placed them on the table "Who's this " Nickko eyed, Russel.

"None of your business " Irma snapped.

A scowl appeared on Nikko's face.

"That's rooster Irma's school slave" Tania mispronounced Russel as rooster "Rooster? Hmm, nice name," Nickko chortled.

"Can I go now," Russel asked head bowed like a loyal servant.

"Yeah, you can leave" Irma dismissed him.

"Hold up" Nickko stopped Russel before he could step away.

"Y.ye..yes" he stuttered.

"So I see you're Rooster, what's your full name" Nickko probed.

"Russell Penn….," Russel replied.

"Russel leaves here this instant" Irma butted in glaring hard at him.

Russel made to leave again, but Nickko held him back by his hand.

"No, I'm not done talking to you, mmm… "you're cute" Nickko licked his lips staring lustfully at Russel.

That look made Russel cringe uncomfortably, seriously a guy was checking him out that was more than awkward

"I'm warning you Nickko leave him alone" Irma snapped temper rising.

"He's just a school slave Irma, you would mind if I have him for the night" Nickko grinned at Irma.

Sighing, Irma lifted her shirt revealing the gun that was tucked in her pants "You still wanna have him for the night?" Irma cocked her brow.

Weeing the gun, Nickko left Russell's hand immediately, or else, Irma might just blow up his head.

Russel's eyes went wide seeing the gun, he had never seen a real gun and so not up close like this. Cold sweats appeared on his forehead.

"Nah I was just playing around….go on ahead Russel " Nickko chuckled nervously.

Without being told twice, Russel practically ran from there. Irma was more dangerous than he thought, she even brought a gun to school.

CHAPTER 6: NOT SO FAST CUTIE

"Haha, you seem like you saw someone killed in front of you" Shaun chortled.

Settled at a booth, Russel told him about what he saw. And surprisingly, to Russel, Shaun laughed.

"What, it's not funny..that was a real gun" he huffed.

"Tsk tsk you're still new Russ, wait till you see Irma point a gun at a teacher then you'll be more surprised " Shaun piqued Russel's curiosity.

"What do you mean" Russel inquired.

"Let me tell you a little something about Irma…she's a mafia girl, deals with guns and hard drugs, kills like it's fun, maybe killing is fun to her" Shaun shrugged.

Russel's blood ran cold, Irma a mafia girl?

Russel has read books about how dangerous mafias are and getting to know Irma as a mafia girl sent chills down his spine.

As a typical wuss and mama's boy, Russell began fretting and began imagining weird scenes.

"Don't fret it, Russ, you're safe as long you don't piss her off" Shaun without waiting for his reply continued "so you saw Nickko check you out"

Coming out of his stupor, Russel replied" yeah, I'm still bizarre about the way he stared at me like I was some chunk of meat."

Helplessly shaking his head Shaun sighed "Nickko is really a pervert both to boys and girls."

He continued: "I think he fancies you now, you know he's bisexual, you better stick close to Irma she's the only one who can save you from him."

"Nickko is bisexual, Ewww that's nuts" Russel scrunched his face in disgust.

"Yeah, he's disgusting."

Irma was done with her food, she got up from the booth and strutted to Russel.

She tapped his head and ordered him to follow her. Saying bye to Shaun, Russel followed her. He held her bag strolling behind her. They walked past their next class.

"Um…ma'am" Russel got startled by how fast she turned to him

"What" she snapped.

Lowering his gaze, Russel probed "we just passed my next class, I need to attend it"

"No, you're coming with me, and don't call me ma'am, it irritates me."

Irma resumed walking, having no choice, Russel followed.

He never thought he'll bunk class, although he didn't do it willingly, what if his parents get to know about it?

His thoughts were short-lived as they've gotten to Triple Threatz's private classroom.

Meliana was seated but Tania wasn't in, a teacher was in.

He stopped when Irma and Russel came in.

Irma eyed him and he resumed teaching, Irma settled in her seat but Russel remained standing not knowing what to do.

"Where you've been, class started a while ago" Meliana mouthed.

"Had to bring my helper along" Irma mouthed back.

"Hmmm, guess you had," Meliana added.

"Ladies…could you please concentrate " the teacher called their attention

"Zip it Scot " Irma snapped at the teacher.

Helplessly shaking his head at her rudeness, the teacher continued his work.

The teachers can't do anything about her rudeness, who would want to get on the bad side of a mafia girl?

"I guess you prefer standing to sit " Irma inquired of Russel.

"Huh.."Russel said in confusion.

"Find somewhere to seat and not hang around like a tree" Irma snapped at him.

Settling on a chair, Russel paid attention to the teacher. But as for Meliana she was doing her nails and didn't seem bothered about the teacher.

Irma was bored of the class and yawned at intervals, crossing and uncrossing her legs.

Halfway through the class, Irma got thirsty and ordered Russel to get her water.

Russel rushed to the cafeteria and bought a bottle of water. Rushing back to the private class he got pulled into a corner and a hand went over his mouth.

"Hello, again nerd" Nickko grinned.

Russel gasped, and Nickko left his mouth.

"What are you doing let me go" he struggled to get away from him.

"Nah Nah…not so fast cutie" Nickko ran his hand through Russel's hair.

"Ah get your disgusting hand off me"

"You better be nice and obedient, no one will save you from me and I can do whatever I want….." Cold metal touched Nickko's neck and he froze.

"What did I say about leaving the nerd alone" Irma's rage was evident in her voice.

"I swear I wasn't gonna do anything to him, I only wanted to talk" Nickko blabbed.

"Drop him" Irma ordered.

Nickko left Russel and he ran to hide behind Irma.,

He gasped, seeing Irma pointing her gun at Nikko's head. His heart jammed against his chest with fear

"You know how I hate to be pissed off right Nickko?" She cocked the gun.

Nickko turned sweating "please don't shoot me, I promise to stay away from him."

"You should have done that from the beginning " with that Irma pulled the trigger.

The deafening sound made Russel's heart jump and he yelled, swooning…

CHAPTER 7: OH BABY BOY I'M THE LAW AROUND HERE

Nickko closed his eyes expecting a cold bullet to dive through his skull, but he only heard a glass-shattering sound. Opening his eyes he saw Irma tucking her gun back into her trouser. He looked behind him and saw a shattered window. Irma shot the window instead of him.

"You missed the shot this time, I might not be merciful if this should happen again..... Stay away from me and my nerd, or I might just shoot whatever is in between your legs," giving him a sinister stare Irma grabbed Russel's leg and pulled him along with her.

The poor boy had slumped with fright and shock.

Nickko watched Irma walk away with Russel.

She just called that nerd, 'Her's'. As in she owned the nerd and the nerd belonged to her.

He resolved to never cross-part with the bed again, he doesn't want his .... to be blown off.

"Well, that was a narrow escape from death," Lrma dragged Russel on the floor, all the way to the private classroom, she went in, dumped Russel at a side, and went to her seat.

Tania had gotten to class. Irma rolled her eyes at her, she knows about Tania and Nickko's secret affair and what they did. The previous teacher had left and a female teacher walked in to teach physics. Russel's favorite subject and Triple Threatz's most hated subject. 'Thermodynamics' was the topic for the day. Seeing the weird name, the girls busied themselves with something else. Ignoring them, the teacher taught them that she was only doing her job and she didn't try to scold them. She went on to explain the first law of thermodynamics, and on the second law, Russel then woke up. He remembered the awful sound of the gunshot and his heart swerved thinking Irma actually shot Nickko. He looked around and saw he was in the private classroom, and all of Triple Threatz were seated with a teacher, teaching his favorite subject and topic. He scanned the room for his bag, retrieved it, and brought out his physics notebook wanting to join the class, completely forgetting about the whole Nickko scenario.

"That's all for now, I hope to see your homework on thermodynamics " the teacher rounded up.

"Wow...I enjoyed the class ma'am " Russel had to admit.

He listened through the entire class and he grasped every teaching in his head.

The teacher, just noticing Russel's presence, smiled at him before walking out.

Left with Triple Threatz, his fear crept back in.

"Wow...I enjoyed the class ma'am," Meliana mimicked.

He high-fived Tania as they laughed at Russel.

"Typical of a nerdy ass nerd to enjoy a brain-wrecking subject" Tania added.

Russel lowers his head taking his lips in, maybe he should have said that out loud.

Lrma glanced at him expecting him to talk back at them or give them a savage line but he was just quiet with his head bowed.

"No wonder why nerd has low fashion sense, their thick head is filled with such hard unnecessary stuff," Meliana huffed.

"Well, at least they've got brains, not like some dumb head who only know how to do manicure and sleep around with boys," Meliana and Tania turned to stare at Irma, as she said that.

With a frown, Tania inquired "Excuse me, what's that supposed to mean,"

Irma ignored their piercing gaze.

"I don't know Irma but your comment seemed as if you were referring to us" Meliana folded her arms in front.

Russel silently watched the battering.

"What!! Why would you think I was referring to you both….well unless you both fit in those categories " Irma shrugged.

"How dare you, Irma, you think you're any better than us…well you aren't, you're just a cold-blooded killer" Tania regretted her words immediately cause in the next minute a gun was pointing at her head.

"You wanna say that again…I'm a cold-blooded killer? Yeah, at least I'm brave to hold a gun and point it at someone…….

What about you? The only thing you can point is those boobs of yours and who do you point it at except Nickko " Irma fumed.

"H..how did you know" Tania stuttered.

"I know more than you think babe, tsk tsk just hope you don't get STD from that dude"

Irma added.

"Russel follow me," she commanded, as she walked out without waiting for him.

Russel rushed out leaving the two girls to sort themselves.

He followed behind her, wondering where they were headed and if he should start up a conversation.

He chose the latter

"Um ma'am….." he moved back the moment she twirled.

"Didn't I tell you not to call me ma'am, how hard is it to pronounce Irma."

"Uh. Irma, I wanted to ask a question "

"Go on" she continued walking.

"Umm.. did you really shoot Nickko?" Russel's ears almost fell off when he heard Irma cackle.

"No silly, you think I'll shoot someone just like that" Irma shook her head chuckling.

"Well um, I heard a few things about how you've killed some people" Russel blurted.

"Yes I've killed some people, and it's only because they were bad to society, I mean, would you refuse for a murderer to be killed" Irma inquired.

"No, but you're a murderer too," Russel answered.

"Guess I'm a good murderer, I kill only the bad not the good," Irma replied.

"We have the law, why don't you leave the law to handle the bad guys," Russel questioned.

The moment they got outside the school building to the parking lot, Irma replied:

"Oh baby boy I'm the law around here, and I don't kill all the time only when the situation calls for it……..

Here, those are my homework, make sure to do them all and make me get a perfect score" Irma handed her notebooks to Russel.

"Ok I will, and thanks for saving me from Nickko."

"Catch ya later baby boy" Irma got on her bike and zoomed out of the compound.

Russel smiled watching her drive away, he just had a nice good conversation with Irma without her yelling at him.

Mr. Agalos residence:

"Hey, old man" Irma greeted.

"Good you're back, hurry up and come down, we've got something to discuss " Agalos replied.

"Sure thing old man, be right down with you" Irma skipped up the stairs giddily.

CHAPTER 8: I MADE FRIENDS AT SCHOOL

"What's Poppin old man" Irma crossed her legs on the table inside Mr. Agalos's study.

Agalos reclined on the spinning chair taking a long drag from the joint in his mouth. He did that a few times and Irma grew impatient. "Seriously old man, did you call me here to watch you smoke" her brows lifted.

"There's a mission for you," Agalos said after a long pause.

"Finally, so what's this mission about…is it to blow out a rival or guide an incoming shipment " she inquired.

"Nothing like that, you're the smartest man I have now Irma, all the other men I hired weren't able to do the job."

Irma's interest reached a high peak at that. Without waiting for her reply Agalos continued: "I need you to scour the earth's surface for these two."

He then placed a photo on the table, Irma took it and glanced at it.

It was a photo of a man and woman, probably a couple from their countenance.

"Hmm, why me, can't one of your men do the job."

Agalos shook his head "Nope, their search has been fruitless, I want you to give it a try."

Irma sighed "okay I'm on it, anything else."

"Ehh, you will have your own guards from now on."

"What, what, what for? I don't need a guard or anyone to protect me I can do that myself " Irma rasped.

"Irma I have so many enemies now I'm getting old, their eyes are on the mafia position I own…..

They would want to harm you to get to me and I can't let that happen…you're the only family I have Irma, try to understand " Agalos explained.

"Fine, whatever " Irma stomped out of the room still upset about the new development.

She didn't want guards to follow her everywhere, but her dad wanted to protect her. Sighing she slumped on her bed on getting to her room. She stared at the photo of the couple she was to find. She noticed something about the woman in the photo. Was it just her or did the woman look so much like Russel?

"C'mon Irma they don't look alike, and why are you thinking of Russel? " she tapped her head.

But as it seems, she had no control of her thoughts as she began thinking of him. His cute baby face, shy countenance, really small eyes, cute big nose. She grinned remembering the short conversation they had. She wondered why a boy of his age would be so shy and unable to defend himself. Even if he's shy, at least he should be able to talk back at some peeps.

Dinner time at the Pennington residence:

The clanking of cutleries as they hit the ceramic plates was the only sound heard in the dining until Mrs. Pennington broke the silence.

"So Russel baby tells us how you like your new school and how you've been holding up."

"Um, well the school is nice I love it……and um I made friends at school too" Russel replied pushing the rim of his glasses back to his nose.

"Wow that's good, how many friends did you make."

"Um two"

"Their genders ?" Mrs. Pennington asked again.

"I think that's enough questions Hunny, allow the boy to eat his food " Mr. Pennington butted in.

"Oh, c'mon I just want to know what gender my baby made friends with" Mrs. Pennington whined rolling her eyes.

"I made friends of both gender," Russel added.

"Glad you were able to make friends baby, I hope to meet your friends one day," Mrs. Pennington caressed Russell's cheeks.

The dinner went on in comfortable silence, Russel zoned out wondering why he included Irma as one of the friends he made at school. He shrugged, maybe Irma could come off as an acquaintance, not a friend.

Either way.

After dinner and doing dishes, Russel retired to his room and cross-checked his and Irma's homework before laying on his bed for a night's rest.

CHAPTER 9: THERE'S NOTHING EXCITING ABOUT ME

Irma rode her bike into the school and parked at her usual spot.

"Good morning Irma," Russel greeted walking up to her.

"Morning nerd..good to see you early" Irma turned off her bike and got off the bike.

"Uh-huh, here's your homework, I did it" Russell handed her notebook to her.

"Thanks, nerd, you can head off to class, I see you at lunchtime " she dismissed him.

He nodded then bounced off.

Irma grinned watching him walk away, she regained herself and then headed to the private classroom.

"Hmmm let's find out where you two could be" Irma mumbled to herself running a scan on the photo Mr. Agalos gave her.

The computer would scan for a similar photo on the net. Irma gazed intently at the computer screen waiting for the result of the scan.

Disappointed with the result, Irma rasped: "Seriously they don't have a social media account, who on earth doesn't have a social media account."

The system failed to find any similar photo to the one she scanned.

The easiest way Irma could have found that couple was tracking them through the internet, but as it seems, they don't have any social media accounts, which is going to make it hard to locate them.

"Man, this is gonna be harder than I thought" she itched her head.

"Well this will have to wait, it's almost time for lunch" Irma packed up her things and went out of the classroom.

"So Mr. Pennington can I know more about you," Irma asked Russel, as they both sat in a booth at the cafeteria with their food trays in front of them. Russel paused on his food when Irma suddenly popped the question made.

"Why?" Russel asked.

"I need to know more than your name" Irma replied.

"Um okay, I'm 19 years old….a nerd and only child of my parents"

"Just that"

"Yeah, nothing is exciting about me"

"Well I think you're wrong nerdy, you do have something exciting about you"

"What do I have"

"You are shy and wussy attitude…

Any typical boy wouldn't be so shy as you are and they wouldn't be so weak…

But you, no offense, but you're pretty much a weakling and coward "

"Is it that bad"

"Yes it's really bad and if you're not careful you'll be trampled on by people who you're older than….you need to learn to defend yourself even if you're a nerd."

"I wish I could, I've never been so exposed to the outside world before, so this is all kinda new to me" Russel sighed.

Furrowing her brows Irma inquired "what do you mean by you've never been so exposed"

"I don't know if I can trust you with this"

"Well if it isn't bad as being a cannibal then you can trust me on it"

"I haven't had the chance to walk out in the open since I was born, until now I've always been inside a house"

"Okay so what, you're like rapunzel now...no way dude, I don't believe that"

"Well, you better believe it cause it's the truth….,"

"Hold up, so you're seriously telling me you've been a kind of prisoner your life, how's that possible?"

"Don't know, I'm just glad my parents agreed to let me go to a real school but I guess I have more problems on my hand"

"We'll get back to this discussion later, for now, we have to figure it out to make you less a weakling"

"I'll ask you some questions about how you'll probably react in a dangerous situation," Irma said and Russel nodded.

'Imagine this scenario, you're walking home alone, and then suddenly a dude walks up to you and smacks your ass, what would you do"

"What are the chances of that happening" Russel inquired.

"50/50" Irma replied.

"Well um, if that should happen then I'll run from the scene."

"That could work if you don't get cornered or something… how about this, it's the same scenario only this time the dude has a gun or knife pointed at you,"

"I'll run, isn't that simple?"

"No silly, try running in that kind of situation and I bet you'll be six feet below in some seconds. …

Tsk tsk, what you should do is to try to play along, then distract them somehow, after that you kick or hit them in a vulnerable spot then, that's when you run," Irma explained.

"Oh, didn't know that" Russel mumbled.

"There's so much you don't know nerd, I'm even wondering if you even know how to kiss a girl"

At that Russel's eyes went wide and his cheeks and ears became red.

"Oh my gosh, don't tell me you haven't kissed a girl or maybe a boy before,"

Russel blushed harder.

"Can you please not mention that word"

"What word, 'kiss'?"

Russel nodded, in agreement.

"What if I chose to sing it, like, kiss kiss kiss kiss kiss kiss kiss kiss kiss kiss.." Irma sing sang.

"Please, can you stop it, it's embarrassing."

And, "Not as embarrassing as a boy who hasn't kissed for once in his life"....

CHAPTER 10: TEACH ME TO BE BOYISH

Mr. Pennington drove the rickety old car into the small driveway of their house. The vehicle made loud engine sounds before turning off, such an old car for a modern world. Mrs. Pennington sat in the passenger seat lost in thoughts, worrying about Russel and he was coping with school. Even though Russel had assured her and her husband that he was okay at his new school, she still worried about her baby boy. This would be his first time experiencing real school life so it's only natural for an overprotective mother to be worried about her son.

"Darn this car, you okay hun" Mr. Pennington inquired

"Yeah yeah I'm fine " Mrs. Pennington snapped back to reality.

"Pfft I'm sure you're worrying about Russel, just let the boy be…

He's been locked up with us long enough, let him live his life a little" Mr. Pennington said.

"I know I'm just worried, what if he encounters the mafia men, you know they're still searching for us…… And also my baby is still new to the world, I'm worried about the kind of friends he's keeping….. You know how kids these days can be so rotten, I want to protect my baby from them," Mr. Pennington sighed hearing his wife's worries.

He too was also worried about Russel but not as much as his wife. He understands Russel needs to get a life for himself, but his wife doesn't get it.

"Calm your mind dear, Russel would be fine and if you're so worried about his friends then ask him to invite his friends over for dinner …….. then you can get to know them and stop your worrying "

"That's a good idea but are you sure we should let strangers into our home... We still need to be careful of the mafia " Mrs. Pennington asked

"Forget about the mafia, one of these days they'll find us, and anyway, we can't run from them forever so what's the use."

"No way I'm not letting the mafia take my baby from me and make him their Lord, mafias are too dangerous " Mrs. Pennington snapped.

Mrs. Pennington had always been scared of mafias and the things they do. Mr. Pennington comes from a powerful mafia family, his elder brother was the heir to the mafia and its businesses. Mr. Pennington didn't have much interest in the mafia business, so he let it all go to his brother. Choosing to live a simple, normal, and happy life. But unfortunately, then his brother was assassinated by a rival mafia. His brother at the time he was assassinated didn't have any children of his own, so the next closest heir to the largest mafia throne -in comparison to others- was Mr. Pennington. Not wanting to head a dangerous syndicate plus Mrs. Pennington's fear of Mafias, Mr. Pennington sorted to hide, far away and undercover. To protect himself and his love, and also, his dream family. Back at the mafia, Mr. Agalos had taken over, and he's currently running the mafia, however as it is, he's in search of Mr. Pennington for a reason best known to him and unknown to those.

"Just do what you think is right hon, I'm going in" Mr. Pennington stepped out of the car and went into the cottage leaving Mrs. Pennington in the vehicle

At the school cafeteria, Irma kept on teasing Russel about his shyness and Russel tried a few times to defend himself but flushed.

"Why don't you teach me how to be like every other boy my age instead of teasing me about it" Russel pursed his lips.

"I could do that, but I'm always busy plus wouldn't it be awkward for a girl to teach a boy how to be boyish."

"You're a boyish girl so you can teach me to be boyish," Russel insisted.

"Fine I'll think about it, get to class the break is over" Irma stood up and walked away.

Russel picked up his things before leaving the cafeteria too.

CHAPTER 11: INVITE YOUR FRIENDS OVER

The school bell rings and Russel stepped out of the building along with Shaun. The two were having a conversation about Afro— Americans and Russel got to know that Shaun was an Afro-American. It came as a surprise to him. Though it was quite obvious Shaun was an Afro-American, from his afro hair, caramel skin, and accent.

"Pretty awesome to have an Afro-American friend " Russel fist-bumped with Shaun

"Yeah man, so I've gotta go catch the train, you coming? " Shaun asked.

"Lead the way" Russel replied.

Pennington Residence:

"Mom I'm home" Russel yelled taking off his shoes as he got home.

Mrs. Pennington strutted out of the eye kitchen with a spatula in her hand. She was making gingerbread cakes before Russel came in.

"Oh my baby is home, hmm I missed you… how school today" Mrs. Pennington bombarded pulling and kissing Russell's cheeks.

"It was good mom, now enough of the kisses" Russel lightly pushed his mom's hands from his face.

"Hmph how to mean, you and your dad are both mean to me" Mrs. Pennington huffed returning to the kitchen.

Russel smiled and went up to his room. He freshened up, had a change of clothes, and did his homework. Thought of a few random things (Irma included), and brushed those thoughts off before he was called down for dinner. He settled with his parents in the dining ready to dig into the food before them.

"Hold a second Russ, I've got something to tell," Mrs. Pennington said stopping Russel from taking a bite of his food.

Without waiting for his reply she continued "Your dad and I want to meet and get to know the friends you've made at school…

So we want you to invite your friends over for dinner one of these days"

"Why the sudden interest to know who I keep friends with" Russel inquired

"Your mom is just being overprotective and paranoid, tried to talk her out of this" Mr. Pennington said.

"Ignore your dad, so Invite your friends over okay"

"Well, maybe if they would come"

"Try to make them to" Mrs. Pennington insisted

Russel nodded then went on with his meal, still wondering what's the fuss all about with his mom.

The next day at school, Russel checked the time on his wristwatch, Irma had missed homeroom and first-class and she still wasn't in school. It was time for the second class.

"Hey Russel, c'mon we've gotta go now" Shaun called from across the hallway.

Sighing Russel went to meet him and they both went to their class.

"You go ahead Shaun I'll meet you at the cafeteria, " Russel said to Shaun

"Okay see ya" Shahn walked off.

Russel took the journey to triple Threatz's private classroom just to check if Irma had arrived. He opened the door to the classroom and peeped in. No Irma was in but the other girls were in, Meliana and Tania. Seeing the mean girls, Russel made to close the door quietly and leave.

"Hey stop there" Meliana snapped stopping him on his track.

"Turn around dunce" she yelled again.

Russel gulped hard turning to face them, though his head was bowed. He wanted to run from there, he was too scared to even take a step back. He waited for Meliana to say something but it seemed like she was taking her time.

CHAPTER 12: LICK MY FOOT YOU SLAVE

"If it ain't the dumb ass nerd" Meliana finally said.

Tania cackled watching Russell's frightened expression.

"Gosh are you even a boy, you're so dumb and stupid" she taunted.

"Man, everything about you is sickening gush" Meliana added.

The meanies took turns insulting Russel. He couldn't do anything or say something, he felt too low and vulnerable to say anything.

"Can I go?" he asked almost whispering.

"Actually no, you know what? Come over here " Meliana ordered.

"No, I really need to go" Russel insisted.

"You don't want me to repeat myself nerd, come here" She yelled

Gulping, Russel took heavy steps towards Meliana.

"Now kneel" she commanded when he got to her front.

Russel did as she told and Tania watched with an evil smirk.

"Take off my shoes" Meliana ordered.

Russel did so.

"Take the socks off and then kiss and lick my foot" she added.

Russel almost gagged and throw up at that insane command. Seriously ordering a guy who could be older than her, and even if he wasn't she should have an atom of respect for him.

"I'm sorry I can't do that" he rejected immediately.

"Do it nerd or else" Meliana held a warning stare.

"Go on wimp" Tania kicked his back.

Wincing at the impact of her heel on his back, Russel proceeded to take off the fishnet sock. He had to pull it down from her knee and he felt uncomfortable doing that. Off with the sock, Melania's scaring-looking leg stared at him. Meliana fixed creepy red long nails on her toes.

"Whatcha waiting for nerd kiss my foot, you slave" She smirked at him. Russel's eyes glistened with tears as he bent his head to kiss her foot. He never imagined himself doing this in his entire existence. With his lips just inches from her foot, Russell was hit by a slap on his face. Which blinded him for some seconds, he was then shoved aside as he held his face in pain.

"What do you think you're doing Meliana " Irma roared.

"Oh..he..hey Irma…great to see you" Meliana stuttered quivering.

"I believe I asked you a question Ms. Meliana " Irma cocked her head.

"Uh. I ..um, we… We're just having fun with your dog" Meliana replied.

"What dog? "

"What, we?" Irma and Tania asked together.

"I met Tania and I were just talking to Russel, we thought we should get to know him"

"Why are you involving me, I never did anything to Russel " Tania denied.

"So asking a boy to kiss your foot is part of getting to know him right?" Irma arched her brow.

"I'm sorry Irma, it was just harmless fun" Meliana apologized.

"So trampling on someone's dignity is fun to you Huh? " Irma retorted.

Meliana shook her head frantically, regretting pulling that stunt on Russel. Who knew Irma was so protective of him. Irma turned to Russel, his right cheek had turned red as a result of the slap she gave him. She grabbed him by his collar and dragged him out of the class without saying another word. Meliana breathed out in relief once she was gone. She made a mental note not to mess with Russel, or maybe she would but without Irma catching her in the act.

Irma pushed Russel into an empty classroom and began lashing him.

"What's wrong with you Russel, why are you so dumb... Were you seriously gonna kiss Meliana, is that how much of a wimp you are... Why would you let her trample over you that way..... I know she seems mean and scary to you but you shouldn't be a scary cat around her... Have some respect for yourself, learn how to talk back or if you can't then walk or run from there don't be such a wimp...... She's not a god that you have to kiss her foot so why would you do that just because she yelled at you...... You disappoint me, Russel, okay I know you're not used to people being mean but you better get used to it and learn to defend yourself. .... You're not a baby and neither are you an animal, use your head, you're a nerd, aren't you?... Then try to be smart and learn to stand for yourself, don't be such an adult baby..... You wanted to attend a real school, how would you enjoy your school days if you let someone rule over you and make you do silly things...... Grow up Russ, you're not a baby anymore" Irma finished off.

Russel bit his lips ashamed and speak: "I'm sorry I just got scared with how she yelled at me."

"Seriously, that means people would keep yelling at you that way and you'll chicken out the same way...... Do yourself a favor Russ, grow some wings and learn to defend yourself, no one would do that for you so do it for yourself " Irma advised.

Russel nodded, he got the point. He needed to grow up and not be a cry baby and chicken.

CHAPTER 13: RUSTLE UP YOUR BIG BOY PANTS

"I'm not advising you to become wayward or rough, just be able to defend yourself, you'll be more happy and satisfied with yourself, that's the best gift you can give to yourself" Irma talked on.

While she talked, different thoughts ran through Russell's mind. He was mentally giving himself a beating for being like a chicken. He behaved so cowardly and after Irma had scolded him, he felt really mad with his earlier self. He couldn't believe he had almost kissed Meliana's foot, her stinky scary foot. Good thing Irma came to his rescue in time, No!!, next time he would save himself and hit wait for Irma. This time it would be Russel's power. He imagined saving himself from terrible situations, making comebacks at insults, the opposite of running and hiding. Unknown to him that he had spaced out and smiled to himself.

Irma frowned wondering what made Russel smile "Hey Russ are you okay, what's funny?....hey hey" she snapped and he jolted back to the present.

"Where'd you go" she questioned.

"Nowhere just a random thought" Russel replied.

"I hope you understood everything I told you, or you were randomly thinking all through the time I spoke? "

"Nope I understand, but I'll need a kind of coach who would teach me to be more fierce and like a normal boy."

Russel stared at Irma with big wide eyes.

"That's easy you can ask your friend to help you, you both are boys anyway so it'll be comfortable for you" Irma replied.

"No I want you to be my Defense coach, you'll be a way better teacher than Shaun, and I don't want to pester Shaun with my troubles"

"You know it's pretty cute how you try to persuade me into being a coach for you but no I can't, I've got things to do" Irma refused.

"C'mon please Irma, pretty pretty please" Russel batted his eyes like a girl.

"Stop being cheesy, fine I'll get my schedule together and see what I can do for you….. But be warned Russel, I'm a strict teacher, so you better rustle up your big boy pants, training starts tomorrow" Irms patted Russel back.

"Return to whatever you were doing, I'll see you later" she smirked the began walking away before Russel could reply.

He watched her walk away with a cheeky grin. His likeness for Irma increases every day, it just happens that way. Most peeps she's really scary and mean, but to him, Irma's the nicest person he's ever met, even though she sometimes yells at him. Other than Shaun, she's pretty sweet. Oh anyway, he has to get back to class.

Mr. Agalos Residence:

"Sup old man" Irma crashed into the chair opposite Mr. Agalos.

"How's the search going Irma " he twirled his joint in between his fingers with his usual stoic expression.

"Chill man, I haven't found any leads on them yet…it's gonna take a long while to get them," Irma replied.

"Keep looking, I know you'll find them, you always do."

The corners of Irma's mouth threatened to stretch into a smile on hearing that.

"Hmmm," she hummed instead and took the joint from Agalos.

She smoked it puffing the smoke through her mouth and nose.

"You ain't supposed to smoke that " Mr. Agalos held his palm under his chin.

"Zip it old man, I know what I'm doing" Irma took another drag from the joint.

Then she stuffed the joint back into Agalos mouth and slapped his bare head.

"Catch ya later old man" she giggled and walked away.

Agalos had a slight frown on his face as he rubbed the spot Irma had hit on his head. He adjusted the joint and got back to work. To him, Irma was getting playful, and carefree. Imagine she even slapped her dad's head.

CHAPTER 14: LEARN TO PUNCH

"Eat up baby, I made these all for you " Mrs. Pennington added more food to Russell's plate.

"It's okay mom I can serve myself " he tried to stop her.

"Why to serve yourself when I can do it for you" Mrs. Pennington giggled.

"Serve me instead, I'm your husband and the love of your life anyway," Mr. Pennington said.

"Yeah mum, serve him, I'm okay by myself, plus you're feeding me too much" Russel pursed his lips.

"Pfft, you two are annoying " she faked a frown.

"Um dad can I borrow some pants from you" Russel inquired.

"Why do you need my pants, they won't fit you," Mr. Pennington worried.

"I need it for something important, please I'll return it as soon as possible " Russel begged.

"Okay, get some from my closet when you're done with your food," Mr. Pennington permitted.

"Thanks, Dad," Russel said with a smile.

The next day at school, Russel held the waist of his dad's pants tightly to prevent them from falling from his waist. He had worn his dad's pants to school, even with a double belt the pants kept falling. He looked ridiculous on it. He walked into the school ignoring the stares people gave him as he passed He met Shaun on the way.

With a puzzled expression, Shaun asked "what are you wearing Russ."

"My big boy pants" Russel replied giddily.

"Huh ?" Shaun arched his brows.

"Irma asked me to rustle up my big boy pants, so I wore this one"

Understanding what he said, Shaun tried to control his laughter but lost it

"Hahahaha, dude!!!" He held his stomach laughing….

"What's funny Shaun, why ya laughing," Russel asked cluelessly.

"Irma didn't mean you should wear oversized pants, she meant you should gather courage and strength, but you got it all wrong" Shaun chortled.

"Oh is that so……..well good thing I wore my pants under it, here" Russel took off his dad's pants, he wore shorts underneath them.

"Good for you, but you need to learn the meanings of some phrases," Shaun said.

"I know and I will let's head to class," Russel said in reply.

"Russel it's time " Irma came up from behind Russell.

"Oh!! Guess I'll be going now Shaun, see ya " Russel waved at Shaun following Irma.

Recess:

They arrived at the private classroom and went in. The two mean girls weren't in, bringing a huge relief to Russel. Though the chairs had been moved to a corner of the class and a human-shaped punching bag was in the middle. With mats surrounding it.

"So are you ready to learn how to be a badass?" Irma asked, tossing her bag across the room.

Russel nodded slowly.

"Nah don't be scared, I won't practice on you, but on the punching bag... What I'll be teaching you are how to defend yourself cause you're a chicken, how to use savage lines cause you're dumb... I'll teach you a better sense of fashion, And if possible, maybe how to handle a gun" Irma stretched her limbs.

"But for today we'll learn how to punch, it's a piece of cake..... First; stretch out your hand like you want a handshake, like so" Irma demonstrated.

Russel did the same.

"Curl your fingers except for your thumb," Irma told him.

"Now use your thumb to hold your index and middle finger" Russel did.

"Good, now you turn it then strike, " Irma punched the mannequin and it fell over and stood back.

"See it's easy, how you try"

Russel walked up to the mannequin with his fist folded like Irma had shown him. Then he struck a blow at the mannequin with his eyes closed. He missed.

"Um hello Russel, how do you expect yourself to hit the target with your eyes closed.....

Open them and try again or I'll pluck them out."

Russel tried again, he hit the mannequin but not hard enough to make it fall.

"Okay let's keep trying"

After an hour...:

"You're getting it, Russel, just try to hit a little harder like this" Irma punched the mannequin and it fell.

It stood back up. Russel breathed out and aimed at the mannequin, he launched a blow with all his strength and hit it. The mannequin fell.

"Ahh yes I did it, I knock….." Russel turned jubilating when the mannequin stood up with force hitting Russel on the head.

He dropped to the floor and passed out.

"What!! A mannequin knocked you down?" Irma held the urge to laugh.

CHAPTER 15: SATURDAY SHOPPING

Russel blinked rapidly gaining consciousness, Irma hovered over him. She had a mocking stare.

"You're up from your coma? Darn, that mannequin hit you pretty hard" she chortled

Russel scoffed and got on his feet holding his head.

"I think I've had enough practice today, let's call it a day", he said.

"Oh no mister, you don't make the rules, I make the rules now let's continue from where we stopped…

Here drink this" she tossed bottled water to him.

He sighed and then drank from it. They replaced the bottle cap.

"Take off your shirt " Irma ordered and she took off her shirt. She wore a sports bra underneath.

Seeing her hard abs made Russel turn his face, his ears turned pink

"Ca…can you please put your shirt back on" he stammered.

"Why " she furrowed her brows.

"You..you're making me uncomfortable," he replied.

"Typically, take off your shirt, we've got so much to do and little time left so hurry."

Russel hastily did as she told. He felt exposed with his little pot belly on display. He didn't have a flat stomach nor did he have abs, but he was good with his cute chubby belly.

"Okay this time we'll learn how to dodge blows and Kicks and some few other tricks, ya got that?

Russel nodded.

"Ow ow ow ow….ouch that hurt let me go" Irma winced loudly as Russel held her down

Russel had knocked her down, he crossed her arms behind her keeping her in that position. He chuckled watching her struggle.

"The one and only though Irma had been taken down, what do you have to say for yourself huh" he smirked.

"Get off me dumbo "… He did.

"Phew, you've learned well student, you even took me down sheesh."

"It's getting late, are we done here" Russel inquired

"Yeah let's get going," she replied.

They put on their shirts and exited the class. They strode the hallway in silence until Russel broke it.

"Um Irma, will you be free sometime this week? My mom wants me to invite my friends over for dinner….. and I was thinking if you could come along with Shaun"

"You told your mom you're friend with a dangerous girl?" Irma questioned.

"You may be dangerous to others but to me, you aren't dangerous"….Irma unconsciously smiled at that him at his response. Russel just complimented her and she liked it.

"Hmmm okay whenever the date is I'm always ready " she smiled at him.

"Thanks, so um I'll be leaving then" Russel hesitated to leave.

"Tomorrow's Saturday, meet me at the town's mall, you'll need to change your wardrobe, " Irma said.

"Are we going shopping? But I don't have enough money to shop for new clothes " he made to refuse.

"The bills on my bud, see you tomorrow " Irma left immediately leaving no room for buts and ifs.

Russel sighed, guessing he had no choice.

Irma got home, greeted her old man, retired to her room, and resumed her search for the couple. After hours of fruitless search, she had dinner, freshened up, and changed clothes then she slumped on her bed her thoughts waving to Russel. She chuckled remembering his cute chubby belly, she felt like squishing it. How cute he looked when he blushes and how fast a learner he is. She dozed off thinking of him.

As for Russel, he got home and received his usual welcome from his mom. He then went up to his room and stripped off his clothes, he showered then came out and wore his pajamas. He read his notes a little then meditated on all that Irma taught him. He smiled remembering how he managed to defeat her. His thoughts went on from there. Later on, his mom called him down for dinner.

Saturday at the town's mall:

Russel succeeded to convince his mom to let him go out to meet a friend. He took a cab to the mall and went in, he walked to the male section of the mall. Irma told him to meet her there. He saw her sitting on a couch and going through a magazine like she felt his presence she raised her head and met his gaze. They exchanged smiles and Russel walked up to her.

"Finally you're here "

"Hi," Russel greeted.

"Alright now let's get shopping, I'll choose the clothes for you and then you study how I pick and select clothes okay" Irma instructed. And Russel nodded in agreement.

"Okay let's get to work."

Russel tried on different clothes and Irma did the judging. After shopping, Irma suggested Russel should have a new hairstyle. So they went to a hair salon and Irma helped him choose a style for his hair. The stylist got to work. Russel looked fabulous and brand new after the haircut. He changed into a new outfit and he looked mesmerizing. Irma got lost staring at him. His usual boyish grin made him cuter. After that, Irma helped him order a set of contacts so he wouldn't use glasses anymore. By the time they were done, it was way past noon. They said their goodbyes and then left for their homes.

Pennington Residence:

Russel got home, his parents weren't in sight, they probably were at work. He sighed in relief, he just wanted to go to his room and rest for a while. Before his parents come back he'll be interrogated about his new appearance. The moment he stepped in, he took off his new shoes and admired them.

"Irma sure does have a good taste in fashion " he mumbled.

He lay on his bed, closed his eyes then drifted off to sleep.

Agalos Residence:

Irma sat with Mr. Agalos at the huge dining table having lunch. Originally Irma planned to work while eating but she spaced out and began thinking of Russel instead. She smiled and sometimes giggled to herself. Russel looked really cute after the makeover she helped him do. Mr. Agalos cocked his head staring puzzled at her. He wondered if a screw had gone loose in Irma's head that was making her act weird. He cleared his throat loud jerking Irma out of her thoughts of Russel.

"Have you become a lunatic?" He gave her a hard stare.

"Dad can't I be happy, I don't always have to be though" she replied.

He shrugged.

"Anyway old man, what are the names of the couple I'm searching for" Irma got busy with her laptop and food.

"Oh boy I've forgotten, uh is it, Larry? Or Rudolph," Mr. Agalos itched his head trying to remember.

"Don't bother yourself old man, tell me whenever you remember, no need to stress your old head, " Irma said. Agalos grumbled at his failed attempt to remember. However, their lunch went on.

Pennington Residence:

The rickety old car engine noise woke Russel from his room. He rubbed his eyes and bounced off the bed to go meet his parents. Mr. Pennington assisted his wife with the bags she held while they walked into the house.

"Hey, mom dad you're back, how was your day" Russell greeted grinning when he met up with them.

The bags in Mrs. Pennington's hands fell, and she was shocked as well as her husband.

Russell's grin grew wider when he saw his parents' shocked faces.

"Oh my goodness, RUSSEL!!!!"

CHAPTER 16: RUSSELL SOON TO BE GIRLFRIEND

Russell's grin grew wider seeing his parent's shocked faces. He knew from their expression that he looked different and more mature.

"Oh my gosh is that you Russel " Mrs. Pennington's mouth was hanging.

"Of course mom who else would it be" he rolled his eyes and picked up the grocery bags and headed for the kitchen.

"But how? You weren't looking like this in the morning before you left, how did you get such a makeover?" She followed after him.

"Well, my friend helped me do a makeover and I'm happy about my new look…

I look more handsome right mom" he cocked his head proudly.

"Yeah, you do look handsome and not like my adorable baby Russ" she affirmed smiling.

"But how did you get the money for your shopping expenses," she asked.

"My friend loaned me some money, I'll pay her back later" he half lied.

Irma didn't loan him money, but he was planning to play her back the money or maybe gift her something to show his appreciation.

"So it's a girl that made you have a makeover," his dad said coming into the picture.

"Ooh are you planning to have a girlfriend " his mom added sharing a knowing look with her husband.

Russell's ears turned a light shade of pink at his parent's ridiculous remark

"What!! No, I'm not" he denied turning his back on them.

They seriously thought he wanted to get a girlfriend.

"Why not? You've come of age and I wouldn't be surprised if you feel like getting your own love partner " he shrugged.

"No no you two are getting it all wrong, Irma is just a friend, and…."

"Oh so her name is Irma, so tell us is she pretty?…. she, definitely, must be pretty for you to like her" his mom blabbed interjecting.

"And maybe she's sexy…no?" His dad added making Russel cover his red face.

Just at hearing the word sexy his brain played the scene when Irma was shirtless and just in a sports bra.

Man!! Her hard abs were too sexy for Russel to handle.

"C'mon Russel talk to us, is she a nice girl, good girl, tough girl, badass girl…."

Russel ran from the kitchen avoiding their questions, he breathed heavily trying to get Irma's sexy figure out of his head.

Impossible though, he kept thinking of it.

He got to his room still struggling with his thoughts. Darn his parents for putting him in this situation, they didn't have pity and just kept on teasing him. Anyways dinner time came, Russel was called down and the family began eating in silence that Russel hoped would last. But that silence was cut short by his mom.

"So Russ honey, tomorrow is Sunday and I would love it if you invite your soon-to-be girlfriend over for dinner… It'll be a perfect scene to get to know her…. I've always hoped for the day you would bring a girl home and soon it'll come true" she clapped her hands.

Russel groaned.

"Your mom is right and I would like to know her too, you know you haven't been out in the open for so long so let's see what you'll bring home" his dad added.

"Alright, alright I've heard you now can I eat" Russel snapped.

"Sure my handsome boy" she made to pull his cheeks but he slapped her hands off

"Stop it, mom, I'm not a baby"

"Yeah yeah get all grumpy pfft" she scoffed.

They continued their dinner and when they were done, Russel retired to his room for a night's rest.

The next day:

Early the next morning after Russel had done his morning duties, he picked up his phone and dialed Irma's number. She had sneaked her number into his phone and he found it so he called her through it. She picked on the first ring.

"Sup big boy" she greeted.

"Hey Irma, how ya doing " Russel cleared his throat trying to sound husky

"I'm good, so why did you call me," she asked.

"Um…you do remember I told you my mom wanted my friends over for dinner right… So I was wondering if you could honor my mom's request and come down to our house for Sunday dinner."

"Oh really?" Irma faltered. But inside she was screaming 'Yes'… She has been expecting his call, she really wanted to get to meet his family.

"Please don't say no Irma, my mom's gonna kill me if you do" he exaggerated

"Haha okay I'll be there," she laughed softly.

"Thanks, Irma, so I'll text you the address see you tonight " Russel hung up.

He pumped his fist.

Agalos Residence:

In her room, staring at her gigantic mirror, Irma accessed her outfit. She put on cargo pants and a loose shirt, she washed the dye off her hair revealing her real hair color. Blond thick hair, she tied it up in a high ponytail. She wasn't satisfied with her outfit, she felt like she needed to wear a dress or maybe a skirt. But the two girls' clothes she hated were dresses and skirts, but she didn't want Russel's parents to have a bad opinion of her. Sighing she searched for a dress or skirt in a closet. She did find a knee-length tennis skirt. She stripped off the cargo pant and wore the skirt and some trainers. Well, it seems like this one looked cute and girly on her. After finishing dressing up, she picked up her phone and bag and then exited the room. She headed down the stairs just in time to see Mr. Agalos coming in with his guards. His eyes almost popped out seeing Irma in a skirt. He can almost certainly say this was the first time he saw her wearing a skirt. Even when he adopted her she wore pants.

"Irma what are you up to" he inquired.

"I'm going out for a while, I would be home late so have dinner without me, bye old man" she skipped past him.

She got on her bike and turned on the Gps on her phone, she then navigated the way to Russell's house.

Once she got there she texted Russel. Irma stood nervously on the front porch waiting for Russel to open the front door. She prep talked herself not to feel nervous but it wasn't working. Shaun just arrived at the house and walked up to her. They said a few Hellos and then continued their wait. Soon enough Russel opened the front door. His eyes beamed and glinted with excitement at the sight of Irma.

"Wow you're here…and you look… gorgeous " he whispered the word loud enough for Irma to hear.

"Oh don't be silly, I'm nothing near gorgeous" Irma blushed lightly.

"No you really are" he insisted.

Shaun cleared his throat loudly breaking the awkward stare between Irma and Russel.

"Russel my man you look….better and your hairstyle is dope" he commented.

"Thanks, Shaun, come in already " he ushered them in.

He led them past the living to the kitchen where his parents were.

"Mom dad meet my friends. Shaun and Irma meet Mr. and Mrs. Pennington " he introduced.

"Hello ma'am" Shaun greeted while Irma waved shyly.

"Aww so I finally get to meet you, Hello Irma, Russel has told us so much about you" Mrs. Pennington pulled her into a hug.

Irma cast a questioning stare at Russel.

He shrugged.

"Nice to meet your future daughter In- law," Mr. Pennington said.

"Urgh Irma don't listen to them, they're just babbling nonsense, come sit here" Russel pulled her from there and help her pull sit at the dinner.

"You're really pretty Irma, no wonder Russel likes you" his mom talked further.

"Uh mom you've said enough why don't you go check the chicken ballotine in the oven, quick shuu, get out of here " Russel chased his mom

Irma chuckled biting her lips.

Does Russel really like her? Shaun settled at the table too along with Mr. Pennington. Mrs. Pennington came back with a tray of freshly baked Chicken ballotine. Irma licked her lips at the delicacy.

"Okay everybody let's dig in"

Russel helped serve Irma making sure she tasted each food set on the table.

"So Irma can you tell us more about yourself," Mr. Pennington asked.

"I'm Irma Agalos and I attend the same school with Russel and Shaun, we recently became friends " Irma replied.

"Hmmm and you managed to get him to like you in such a short time, you would believe how much he talks about you at home " Mrs. Pennington.

But inside she knew Irma's surname sounded familiar but she brushed off the thought.

"Urgh mom will you please stop lying, I've never talked about Irma" Russel groaned

Irma smiled.

"Well thanks for making our son make good changes and we hope to see more of you," Mr. Pennington said.

Irma nodded, she sneaked her phone out of her bag under the table.

At this point, it becomes too clear to ignore. She opened her gallery and tapped on the couple photo who she was searching for. She almost gasped loudly realizing the couple in the photo was sitting opposite her. The couple was Russell's parents and she was having dinner with them.

Seeing her change of expression Russel inquired "are you okay Irma "

"Oh yes I'm fine, the food is really delicious " she composed herself and kept back her phone.

The dinner continued with Russel getting teased by his parents and Irma laughing. Shaun almost felt invincible but he was involved in some of the conversations. At exactly 10:00 they were done and ready to leave.

"Bye Irma, come again soon " Mrs. Pennington waved.

"I will, thanks for the dinner" Irma replied.

Russel escorted her and Shaun outside the house. Shaun said his goodbyes and left in a cab. So at this point, it was just Irma and Russel alone.

"So about what my parents said in there, don't mind it they just made it all up" Russel itched his head.

"Hehe it's nothing I actually enjoyed the chats, and your mom is really nice," she said

"Thanks for coming. …" Russel trailed off not knowing what else to say.

"I'll see you tomorrow big boy, good night," she said and suddenly pecked his cheeks.

He gasped turning red. Irma chuckled and got on her bike, she wore her helmet the zoomed off. Still in shock, Russel touched the spot her lips kissed. He blushed so hard and felt hot. All through her ride home, Irma thought of how weird it was that the couple her old man wanted was Russell's parents. The only thing is that she doesn't know why he wants them to be found.

CHAPTER 17: SHE WANTED A FAMILY

Irma parked her bike in the huge Garage, she turned it off, got down then tossed the key to the bike to a guard who stood nearby. He caught it and bowed in respect. Ignoring him she walked into the house (More like a mansion than a house), the living room was a little dimly and a few guards were positioned in different corners. They bowed in respect when they saw her, she was almost their boss and they were under her. Some of them had undergone training through her so she deserved the high respect which they gave her. Her dad wasn't in sight so she took the stairs to her room. She got in and slammed the door shut. She sighed heavily and proceeded to change her clothes. She took out a pair of PJs and began stripping, she took off her shirt first and her stuffed belly bulged out. Mrs. Pennington did well to overfeed Irma and her flat stomach bulged up with food. She didn't complain each time Mrs. Pennington filled her plate with food, instead, she smiled heartily and ate with relish. She felt more at home with them than she ever had, she felt loved and cared for by Russell's mom. And, somehow a deep sadness rose from within her, she wanted what Russel had,.....A Mother's Love!! Within a few hours, Mrs. Pennington showered her with love and care. She welcomed her with a hug and smile which warmed Irma. She never felt like that, her old man would just nod at her whenever she got back home and it almost seemed like he didn't love her. But he did, but as a mafia lord, he didn't have time for showering affection or anything of that sort. Well since Mrs. Pennington already told her she could come over anytime she wanted and could even stay overnight then she was good with that. The woman was really nice and to think she believes she would become Russell's girlfriend. She laughed replaying the scene in her head of Russell's parents teasing him and he tried to make Irma not take to heart what they were saying. Russel looked cute and adorable with the helpless expression he had in front of his parents. Sighing again she wore the PJs.

"Must be nice to have a real family" she thought.

She got in bed and began daydreaming unconsciously about Russel. Since he came into her life things have been changing, most especially for her. She was never really nice and she didn't care about others or even tried to help. But now, she felt like she should be nice more often, she wanted to be less frightful and more approachable. Maybe she might want to do this for Russel but she also wanted to do it herself. She wants to be a better version of herself. And then she remembered the assignment her old man gave her. She found the couple but then they were parents to someone close to her. How was she gonna deal with this?

On one hand, she was happy that she could finish her assignment….. and on the other hand, Russell's parents would be in big trouble if her old man wanted them to finish them off. It made her wonder what connection they had with her old man. Because they seemed like real ordinary people, why was her old man after them? She fell asleep late.

Irma left for school early the next day and met up with Russel. He dressed impressively and Irma may have drooled over him a little. She was proud of her work at least she'll get to look at a cute handsome face every day. How naughty of her. The day went by fast without much trouble, they went their ways and Irma was back in the house. Mr. Agalos was waiting for her return, he was eager to hear about her progress in the search. Time was running out and he needed to sort things out fast. Soon enough Irma came in grinning widely, and surprisingly she wore a skirt again today. He watched as a guard went over to call her to come to meet him. She walked over and greeted him.

"Sup old man" she slumped into the chair beside him.

He grunted a reply.

"How far have you gone with your search" he wasted no time in asking.

"I'm getting close, soon enough I would get them" she replied.

"How soon?" He questioned.

"Really soon, but eh….." she hesitated to ask him what was on her mind.

Sensing her uneasiness he prompted her to go on.

"Dad, you haven't told me the reason why you want me to search for this couple…… and you didn't even give me their names, be clear on why you want me to find them" she let out.

Mr. Agalos stared at her wondering if he should tell her. This was a confidential matter and needed to be handled with care. He couldn't let any slip-up mess up his plans. But then Irma was his most trusted person, he could tell her….right?

CHAPTER 18: HISTORY OF THE PENNINGTON'S, BRAND NEW RUSSEL

After god what seemed like forever, Mr. Agalos opened his thin lips and then asked: "why are you interested to know about them."

He had no expression on his face and was just blank.

"C'mon old man, tell me their connection to you, and depending on how important they may be then I put in more effort" Irma tried to coax him.

He hummed, arching his brows, he took his time to pause at each word as he spoke: "the couple I want you to search for is very important people to the mafia community........They are Larry and Sabrina Pennington, they're the only remaining defendants of the Pennington family....... The late Pennington couple held a high position in the mafia realm and they governed this mafia and built it up to the highest...... They had two sons, Osmond was the elder one and Larry was the younger....... Osmond loved the mafia life and spent his youth learning and training himself in the mafia way, he wanted to rule the mafia and his father was pleased with him........ As for Larry, he didn't like the mafia as much as Osmond did, so he never paid attention to Osmond's quest to take over the mafia....... Their parents died and willed the mafia to Osmond, he was happy and ruled the mafia better than his father did.......... He didn't acquaint himself with any women so he didn't have a child of his own. I know all this because I was friends with Osmond........ Men from a rival mafia assassinated Osmond and wanted to seize the throne. I had to step in to keep the mafia in order on behalf of my best friend......... Logically Larry would be the one to take up the mafia throne but he was dating Sabrina then, she hated the mafia and their ways and was against Larry heading the mafia....... Larry wasn't interested in the mafia from the start so he handed it to me and then fled with Sabrina....... I couldn't let all the hard work of my friend go to waste or go to the rivals so I became the Drug Lord of the Pennington's mafia........ But now I would need to retire soon as I'm getting old, so the reason for my search is to get Larry to run this mafia...... If he can't then he should have a son or a descendant of his to pass the mafia to...... Larry never had what it takes to run a mafia, he was always a soft boy and I doubt he'll take it on now....... And that's why he's hiding from me, so now I've told you everything. Will you hasten your speed in finding them ?" He inquired.

"So you're not planning to hurt them, you just want Mr. Larry to take over the mafia?' Irma questioned.

Without waiting for him to reply she continued " if you found out where they are today what will you do."

"Let's get them first then we'll talk about it" he made to brush off the topic.

"Um...I've actually found them and I know where they are," Irma said quickly.

He cocked his head "really?"

Irma nodded, then proceeded to tell him about Russel, how she went to his house for dinner and found out his parents were who her old man wanted. At the end of her revelation, Anglos had an unreadable expression but in the next moment, he roared in laughter. The room reverberated with the sound of the thick hoarse laugh. It wasn't a laugh of mockery, but a laugh of victory or something of that sort.

"Ahh finally I found you, your rat hole has been dogged up, Larry, prepare yourself. ….

Good job Irma, you'll need a raise" he patted her hair.

Irma forced out an awkward smile

"So, what will you do now" she wanted to ask but he already left.

She hoped in her heart she hadn't made a mistake by telling him where Russell's parents were. Although she hadn't told him their address yet he would still ask for it. Well, he has assured them he wasn't planning to hurt them so she could rest assured they'll be safe……right? She wouldn't want Russel to lose his parents because of her.

Next day at the Pennington residence:

After Russel left for school with the package that his mom had made for Irma, the couple left for the local market to sell off some goods. That was how they sustained themselves and managed to send Russel to school. They wrapped up for the day when they were done and then headed home. Larry turned off the car engine once he drove into the driveway and then got down. He and Sabrina walked to the front of a door and made to unlock it when they realized the door was open. They exchanged puzzled glances.

"Is Russel supposed to be back from school by this time?" he asked

Sabrina shook her head.

Maybe Russel had come home early. With that in mind, they went in only to see. Mr. Anglos along with his men comfortably sitting in their living room.

Recess At School, private Classroom:

Amid perspiration and grunting, two people struggled against each other. They each tried to bring the other down but they both stood their ground and refused to surrender. He blocked her blows but refused to retaliate, he didn't want to hurt her so he just let her attempt to punch him. While she tried to hit him, she also waited for him to strike at her but he didn't. Suddenly he knocked her down, turned her over, and sat on her back. With his voice hoarse and deep Russel asked "Irma aren't you tired yet let's take a break." Her eyebrow furrowed in puzzlement. She blinked to make sure she just heard Russel talk and not an impostor. He saw her weird facial expression " what's wrong with your eyes." This time Irma was sure Russel was the one talking but his voice was deep and more manly. His voice seemed to have developed a kind of aura and power that made her insides churn in excitement. Usually, his voice was always high-pitched like a tween and she sometimes doubted the age cause of his voice but now. He sounded sexy? …..mature?…..powerful?…..royally?….. She couldn't find what word to describe but one thing was sure, she liked this new voice. And she wished it'll be permanent and not because of the exercise they just did.

"Russel gets off me, you're gonna choke me with your weight " she snapped.

He stood immediately.

"Did you eat something weird or perhaps took alcohol yesterday?" She couldn't stop herself from asking.

He shook his head before saying" nope just my mom's usual home-cooked meal and for alcohol? I've never tasted that stuff so……" he shrugged.

Irma's eyes lit up the moment she heard him say he's never tasted alcohol. A sly smile appeared on her face like a mischievous fox.

"Let's take a break"

She opened her bag and took out two bottled water. She tossed one at Russel. He opened it and began taking huge gulps from it. Irma forgot to drink from her bottle and focused on his Adam's apple. She watched it move up and down as he drank from the bottle. A few droplets of water spilled from his mouth and trailed down his throat and into his chest. Her eyes grew wide and she began biting her finger and slowly a surge of redness rushed to her cheeks. In all of history, it hadn't for once been rumored that Irma Agalos fancied a boy and even drooled while watching him.

It almost seemed like she was gay. But right now, watching a nerd boy drink water, Irma was ogling, drooling, and blushing at him. This has got to be the Guinness world record. Suddenly Russell's gaze swept past her and she got back to her senses. She turned on a nonchalant expression and acted like, she didn't almost eat him up with her eyes. But the honey glow was still in her cheeks.

Russel furrowed his brows at her "what's up with your cheeks? It's all red."

She felt her cheeks with her hand and indeed they felt hot. "I'm not blushing… it's just normal for my cheeks to get red when I'm hot and sweaty… I wasn't staring at you……. Why would I even stare at you?… you're not sexy, maybe you are a little bit but I wasn't staring at you…." Irma gasped realizing she's been blabbing nonsense and unknowingly admitted she found Russel sexy.

She immediately tried to save herself from embarrassment "ignore whatever nonsense I just spurted….. And don't even dare to think I find you sexy, I would never fancy any boy." She wanted to make Russel ignore whatever he heard but it sounded like she was convincing herself that she didn't just drool over a nerd. She wanted to shoot herself or hug a flammable cylinder to ease the embarrassment she felt. She stole a glance at him, he was smiling at her. What did he think of her now? A weirdo?…blabber beak? ….lunatic?…. Tons of nonsensical thoughts ran through her mind at that moment.

"Meet me at the front gate before you go home" with that said she rushed out of the class.

Leaving Russel dumbstruck with just a curved-up lip. Irma's cheeks were so red that they looked like blood would seep through them. He had the urge to pull and rub her cute cheeks

But what made him dumbstruck was the fact that Irma checked him out and even drooled. He chuckled to himself watching her silhouette disappear from his sight.

……At exactly 4:30 pm when the electric school bell rang, Russel stood at the front gate waiting for Irma. He had sent Shaun and missed the train that would have taken him home just so he could wait for her. He held the package his mom made for Irma. He held his curiosity and didn't peek into the package. Soon enough Irma drove her bike out of the school and stopped a few meters from him. She gestured for him to come over. He did and she handed a helmet to him.

"Put it on and get on let's go," she said leaving no room for excuses.

He looked hesitant but he wore the helmet over his head. He handed the package to her and told he it was from his mother. She smiled and then kept it in her bag. He then got on the bike behind her.

"Hang on" she sped off causing shock to Russel as he almost fell off the bike.

He immediately held onto her in panic with his hands around her stomach. Irma's eyes widened under the helmet and she lost control of the bike for a moment. They almost crashed into a car in front. Thankfully she gained control and drove them safely to her destination without either of them getting killed. She breathed out once she parked then she tapped Russel to get down. He had been in a daze all through the ride, he opened his eyes and took his hands off her body then he climbed off the bike. He took in their surroundings and realized they were at a pub. His brows scrunched up in confusion and he cast a questioning stare at her.

"What are we doing at a pub"

She took off the helmet and then turned off the bike before turning to reply to him: "you mentioned you haven't tasted alcohol before…..

Well, a few moments from now you will be drowned in alcohol " she pulled him into the Pub before he could digest what she said.

CHAPTER 19: HIGH ALCOHOL TOLERANCE

Larry and Sabrina shook their heads to clear off whatever illusion they were seeing. But Agalos still sat there, on their couch and he had a sinister smile on his face. Sabrina tightened her grip on Larry's hand due to fear. They'd been found by who they were hiding from. It was enough to send chills down her spine. But how did Agalos find them? What will he do with them? Will he kill them or take them captive? Larry was no different, he pulled Sabrina into his embrace to protect her. He tried to put on a brave look but he still had fear in his eyes. He knew Mr. Agalos had two motives to find him. To either kill him so the mafia would permanently become his or to force him back into the mafia. Mr. Agalos sat crossed legs with a rolled-up joint in between his fingers. The white smoke from the joint butt spread through the air and Sabrina coughed the moment she inhaled it. Agalos's smile stretched across his face. He stood up and then took slow rigid steps toward them. They seemed to be in a staring competition as neither of them broke the stare. While different questions and fears ran through Larry's and Sabrina's heads, Mr. Agalos was joyful in his successful attempt to get them. Heaven knows how long he's been searching for them, and today he'll wipe them off the surface of the earth. Yeah, he would make sure of it, nothing would stop him now. He has waited long enough for this moment and it's finally time. Larry held Sabrina tight and retreated with each step Agalos took toward them.

"What's wrong Larry, surprised to see me?" Mr. Agalos stopped in his tracks having an evil glint in his eyes. `

"What are you doing here Agalos, how did you find us?" Larry questioned.

"Is that how to greet an old friend, not an ounce of hospitality?.....

Hah, that's not fair" Mr.Agalos' expression switched from being sinister to upset then back to sinister.

His glare made Larry and Sabrina squirm, she tugged on Larry's shirt. His eyes turned dark and one couldn't tell what he was thinking.

"Old friend we will get to talk and catch up later, get'em boys" he snapped his fingers, and his men charged toward Larry and Sabrina.

"Hurry let's get out of here" Larry pulled Sabrina with him as they raced out of the house with Agalos men chasing behind them.

"Don't let them get away"

The men caught up with them in no time.

"Ugh let me go, let go" Sabrina struggled with them and her neck was twisted immediately.

She fell unconscious.

Mr. Agalos. came out of the house with an evil grin on his face.

"Did you really think you could hide from me forever?.... Surely you didn't, but I must say, you really did hide for a very long time, and I'll do well to repay the favor."

With a command, Larry and Sabrina were hurled into one of the cars and the doors were shut tightly. Mr. Agalos smirked, satisfied, then got into the front car. The driver began driving away immediately.

Somewhere in El Paso:

A man rushed into the study stumbling on his foot, he fell in front of his master. He seemed like he had a very important message to pass and he couldn't wait to say it.

"Go on" his boss only spared him a glance before turning back to the stripper who was entertaining him. The assistant wasted no time saying, "the last descendant of the Pennington has been found……" His boss had already stood up in rage before he could finish his sentence.

"What!!! They're still alive?"

The assistant gulped fearfully before continuing "Yes boss, there's indeed a descendant of the Pennington's left"

"Where is he?" His boss calmed down.

"We recently got his location, but Agalos was faster than us and he has him in his custody " the assistant replied.

"Ooh Agalos has interfered in my plans of gaining acquisition of the Pennington mafia time and again,… Keep an eye on Agalos and capture that last descendant of the Pennington, nothing will stop me from getting the mafia" the man said his dark eyes sending chills to his assistant.

"Yes, boss I'll get our men on it" the assistant rushed out.

Pub:

Russel eyed his surroundings and felt choked up. It wasn't a club, just a bar but he didn't like the smell of alcohol and cigarettes. Irma pulled him to a stool and sat him down before he could protest.

She called for the ban…."2 shots of vodka" she ordered.

"Irma, what are,e we drinking for?" Russel asked.

"Chill Russel it's about time you try something new" she brought out a pack of cigarettes from her bag and took out a stick.

She placed it in between her lips and was about to lightweight when Russel took the stick from her lips and threw it away. He also seized the pack from her.

"You know smoking is harmful, right?"

"I do" she snapped and tried to get the pack from him.

"You do and you still smoke, I don't think you want to age faster or get lung cancer or tongue cancer, or stomach cancer……." Russel went on listing to list the advantages of smoking.

And when he was done Irma had a look of fear in her eyes. She knew the consequences of smoking but, she just can't help it. She's not an addicted smoker so she didn't think it would affect her. But now that Russel mentioned it she became afraid and cut him off

"Okay I've heard you, and I won't smoke anymore, okay?."

The barman placed the two glasses of vodka in front of them. Irma grabbed one and chugged it down then gestured for Russel to do the same.

"Um, I don't think we should do this, what if you get drunk ?" He hesitated to drink it

Irma rolled her eyes and then order another shot.

"I have high alcohol tolerance I won't get drunk easily so relax" with that said she chugged down another glass.

Russel brought the glass up to his lips, and he sniffed in the hard smell of the drink. He took a tiny sip of it and dropped it down in disgust. He glanced at Irma and saw that she looked funny. She had just drunk the third glass and she was feeling tipsy. So much for someone with high alcohol tolerance. Her head swayed from side to side as she ruffled her hair.

"Argh… Russel what did you put in my drink, I feel tipsy already"

"Me?" He asked wondering when he added something to her drink.

"I know you like me but you shouldn't spike my drink ……

You're a bad boy, you made me drool and stare at you when I shouldn't have…..

You're so cute and I couldn't stop staring at you, I even blushed haha" she laughed hysterically losing control of herself.

Russel held the urge to laugh at her silliness...

Somewhere in Tijuana/Mexico:

"So what's Agalos latest move," A man asked.

His dark eyes gave an aloof and cold aura to those around him. His custom-made suit gave him an elegant look and along with his cold demeanor gave his subordinates chills and they dreaded upsetting him. The smell of cigars and alcohol with a stash of cocaine on the table. The room was dim-lit and the sun rays seeped into the room through the closed curtains and reflected on his face. The fine lines of wrinkles and a sturdy mustache.

"Um, Irma Agalos was able to find the last descendant of the Pennington and Agalos has taken them hostage...... We haven't got any other plans of his from our insider and where he kept them hostage is unknown........ And also the other mafia from El Paso are after ``The last Pennington" his assistant filled him in on the details.

"Hmmm, watch their every move and don't miss out on anything..... It won't be too long before the Pennington fortune would become ours" he said pausing at each word.

"Yes master" his assistant bowed respectfully.

He then left the sturdy.

Back in Mazatlan/Mexico, at Agalos' residence:

"Take them down to the basement boys" Mr. Agalos ordered and followed behind his guards as they took Larry and Sabrina to the basement.

The trap door that led to the basement was opened and they took stairs down into the basement. Larry kept struggling to get out of the grips of the men... Fat chance Sabrina was still unconscious so little struggle came from her. Larry was hurled into the room and Sabrina was thrown at him. He picked her up and checked her pulse. Thankfully she was alright, he sighed in relief. He turned to glare at Mr. Agalos.

"What's the meaning of this? Why did you abduct us?" Mr. Pennington questioned in anger.

"Haha, do you dare to ask that question?...... You should know your brother and my best friend left the mafia in my hands and I rule over it….."

Larry cut Agalos off before he could finish: "The mafia is yours, I don't want it why do you still pester our life."

At this moment, Mr. Agalos ordered his men to leave the basement. He walked to a corner and retrieved a box, he opened it and took out two syringes. A blue liquid was in them.

He saw the look of fear in Larry's eyes and smirked: "Yes you're right, the mafia is in my hands but it's not fully mine and that's because you're alive... The entire Pennington lineage must be cut off before I can fully gain control of the mafia….. You see I've got a gift for you and your dear wife, this syringe would give you a peaceful death, no pain or torture...... You'll fall unconscious then die and the mafia would be all mine haha" Agalos eyes had an evil glint as he laughed.

He strolled toward Larry still having that sinister stare. Larry moved back and shielded Sabrina from him.

"Stop this Agalos, I have no intentions of taking the mafia from you, please leave us alone" Larry pleaded.

Those pleas fell on deaf ears as Agalos pulled him from Sabrina.

"Well, friend you should be happy I'm willing to give you a painless death" Agalos stabbed him in the shoulder with the syringe.

Larry groaned too weak to fight Agalos off. The blue liquid entered his bloodstream. He felt his head burning, his eyes rolled to the back and he went listless. Still, like a dead man, Agalos smirked, satisfied then, he went for Sabrina, he injected her with the liquid too. He then dragged their bodies and placed them in a minecart. He pushed the cart into an open door and the cart began drifting away into the underground tunnel. He shut the door and then locked it. He threw the keys into a burning furnace and then left the basement. The only hindrance to his success has been wiped off.

CHAPTER 20: BELIEVE ME

"You know what? when I first saw you I thought you were a dumb nerd… You looked so frail and weak like a premature baby….who knew you would become so hot that you made me drool over you… Haha Russel you're a bad boy, do you know you have broken a record…hmmm?…… I know you don't know why you are so handsomely adorable, I feel like squishing your soft cheeks and pulling your hair…… I have a high alcohol tolerance and I won't get drunk even if I drink ten bottles….. See I'm not drunk yet but I do feel a little dizzy and my vision is blurry….."

Russel watched Irma ramble on and on.

First, she praised him, and now she raised herself. Who knows what else she'll talk about? He stood up from the stool and held her shoulders

"C'mon Irma, you have enough already, we need to leave now"

She pursed her lips having a frown on her face "No I don't wanna leave yet, we still need to have more fun."

Russel sighed, the tough Irma has turned into a child throwing a tantrum.

"We can have fun when we get home" he tried to placate her but she didn't move a muscle.

"Do you want a Popsicle or some vodka gummies?" he asked.

"Yes," Irma replied.

"Yes, for a Popsicle or vodka gummies?" Russel asked.

Gummies… Irma clapped and smiled girlishly.

Russel turned to the bartender and ordered some gummy bears

deepened in vodka. The bartender handed a pack of vodka gummy bears to him. Usually, gummy bears were small and sour candies but this particular has been soaked in vodka for hours so it absorbed the vodka and swelled thrice its usual size. Russel then paid the bills. Then, he held Irma and helped her out of the Pub. They had no choice but to take a cab because Irma was drunk and there was no way either she or Russel could drive without an accident happening. Russel locked Irma in his embrace whilst she kept squirming to get out of his hold. He felt awkward as the driver spared them a glass through the front mirror.

"Irma stop moving, you are embarrassing yourself " he whispered to Irma.

It seemed to work cause she became calm and didn't move. She busied herself with his hand toying with it. She pouted her lips and her cheeks seemed to get red due to her drunken state. The cab stopped in front of Pennington's house and Russel helped Irma out, he then paid the cab man.

He had no idea where Irma lived and even if he knew, he wouldn't dare go there. He might not make it out alive if he goes there. He threw Irma over his shoulders despite her kicking and yelling. Good thing she was wearing pants lest her underwear is exposed. Russel noticed the car wheel tracks on the driveway. Several wheel tracks, his father's old car was parked in the driveway but it's been smashed by Agalos cars. He frowned seeing his mom's flower bed has been trampled on. He wondered what kind of guests his parents were having. Getting to the front door he found it open. His expression turned grim as his brows furrowed. He walked in and dirt patches on the living room floors and a broken flower vase welcomed him. The entire room was silent without a single soul except for him and Irma

"Mom …. Dad" he called.

Only silence replied him.

"Who's your mama cause I ain't your mama" Irma blabbed.

Russel tried to calm himself as he walked further into the living room. He sat Irma on a couch and told her to stay put and she did like an obedient puppy. He ventured into the kitchen and began making a sobering tea for Irma. He allowed it to cool before he went back to her. She had made herself comfortable on the couch and stretched her legs on the table in front of her.

"Here's some tea for you, drink it and I'll give you the gummies."

At the sound of getting vodka gummies, Irma grabbed the cup and chugged down the tea. She exhaled from her mouth and then relaxed her back on the couch, her eyes were closed but she was awake. While she took time to sober up, Russel tried calling his parents. Their numbers weren't going through. His heart accelerated as numerous thoughts ran through his brain. What if his parents went out for a stroll but got into an accident? Or what if they were robbed and his parents were taken away? Or what if…

Irma's voice cut through his thoughts: "Russel what are we doing at your house and why is the place dirty," she asked.

The sobering tea has cleared her drunkenness.

"Nice to see Ms. High alcohol tolerance is back to normal" sarcasm laced Russell's voice.

"Did I get drunk" Irma inquired.

"No, you didn't haha….. isn't it obvious you did?"

"Um….I… I didn't do anything stupid…..right? " she asked.

"We'll talk about that later but right now my parents are missing "

"What do you mean missing, aren't they home?" Irma was confused as much as Russel was.

"Yeah I thought they would, but the house is empty and in mess, and the door was opened and some cars seemed to have been in the driveway" he explained.

"Cars?…" Irma's heart thumbed with the possibility that her old man had visited Russel's parents.

"Yeah in the driveway"

Irma walked out of the house to the driveway. She examined the tracks and her fears were confirmed. The custom-made wheel her old man's car used was tracked on the driveway. It meant only one thing, Agalos has been there and he has taken Russel's parents away. Oh boy!! How would she explain this to Russel?

Would she say "hey Russel my father man appointed me to search for a couple, and the couple turned out to be your parents? … And I told him your address and now he's taken them away to probably kill them?"

She knew she could tell him that but neither could she hide it from him. As much as she hates to admit it, she has a huge hand in their disappearance. With a heavy heart, she walked back inside ready to tell Russel everything. And she did that. She told him how she wanted her to find a strange couple… then how the couple turned out to be his parents, how her old man told her he wouldn't hurt how she gave him their address.

"Trust me, Russel, I never knew he would take your parents away, I thought… I mean he told me he wouldn't hurt them….. If you want we can go over to my old man and ask if about it… but please don't hate me I didn't mean for this to happen" she explained all in one breath.

She anticipated Russell's reply but non come.

"Are you saying your father could possibly have abducted my parents? "Russel asked.

Irma nodded and said "Yeah he is the only person who I told where you live"

"But what would your father want with my parents?" Russel asked, wondering.

"I don't know but he did say he won't hurt them so we can be rest assured they'll be fine" she replied.

Russel stared at the girl in front of him, he could tell she was saying the truth through the look in her eyes. He could see she was scared as much as he was. And he trusted her too.

"Okay let's go see your father, I want to see my parents and be sure they're okay" he stood up front where he sat.

Irma nodded in affirmation and they left the house.

"Oops we left your bike back at the pub so I guess we will have to take a cab," he said and tossed her bike key at her.

Irma nodded, she didn't want to probe further into what nonsense she might have done when she was drunk. They hailed a cab and entered

Agalos residence:

Irma paid the driver and then walked to the front gate of the huge building. A retinal scan scanned her eyeball then the gate opened. Russel gasped behind her. Different mean-looking guards surrounded the area. They had guns and their states were enough to give a weak-hearted person chills. Russel braced up and closely followed behind Irma. He followed her into the vast, beautiful, eerie living room. Irma told him to make himself comfortable whilst she goes get her old man. Russel sunk into one of the sofas and bowed his head. Internally he prayed Mr. Agalos didn't harm his parents. They're the only family he has now. Agalos had a happy expression on his face with his thin lips tugged up. For a man who usually wore a grim face, that look of happiness didn't suit him. He actually looked better with a mean face. One of his plans has been completed. No one would be able to find Larry and Sabrina, he has wiped them off. Thanks to his Irma they won't be a pest to him anymore. Soon plan B will come into action. Thinking of this he roared with laughter. All these riches would be his alone, with no legitimate heir or heiress to share or fight it with. A knock interrupted his thoughts.

Thinking it was a guard he said: "leave me, I didn't send for any of you."

Irma opened the door and stepped in.

Seeing her his eyes brightened but his expression turned cold.

"Old man we need to talk"

"Sure take a seat"

Irma sat and looked him dead in the eyes.

"Why are you looking at me like that," he asked.

"What did you do to the Penningtons?" Irma wasted no time in asking.

"Oh, so this is about the Penningtons, well like I told you I didn't harm them….."

Irma cut him off, saying: "If you didn't harm them, then why are they missing from their home?"

Agalos frowned lightly "how did you know they aren't at their house?"

"They are the parents of my friend, I only told you their address because you promised you wouldn't hurt them" Irma rasped throwing, her hands in the air

"A friend?" he asked.

"Yeah, he's Russel, the son of the Pennington couple you abducted…..

The poor boy has been worried sick about his parents and that's why we rushed down here …… I hope you haven't done anything rash to them" Irma raised her eyebrows slightly. But Agalos completely ignored her and walked out of the sturdy. Irma followed. He got downstairs and found Russel sitting on one of the sofas. He checked out the boy, he had a lot of resemblance to Sabrina. Irma stood beside him.

"This is your friend?" It sounded more like a statement than a question from him.

Irma nodded, and at that point, Russel noticed them and stood from the sofa.

"So old man, where are his parents? what did you do to them?" Irma asked on behalf of Russel.

"Expect the worst-case scenario. ……"

Irma cut him off, not waiting for him to finish his statement, she said: "What!! What do you mean by that"

Mr. Agalos had a look of annoyance and said: "Use your imagination." With that Agalos left there, leaving Irma in a confused state.

Russel walked up to her and asked: "So what did he say, where are my parents"

"I don't know and I don't understand either" Irma replied.

"Is….is it possible that your father has killed my parents" he stuttered.

"Yes, maybe he did, but I know my old man…

If he did kill anyone he would go straight to the point and tell me no matter who the person is… But now he didn't say he killed them neither did he say he didn't" Irma tried to get meaning out of Agalos' words when he said: 'Expect the worst-case scenario' and 'Use your imagination.' Those two sentences could mean anything.

"Are you saying that maybe my parents are still alive," Russel asked his voice full of hope.

"Maybe, ugh, if only that old man could say a meaningful sentence and not leave my head in a whirlwind… Don't worry Russel we'll find your parents okay? I have a feeling that they're alive," Irma held his face in her palms as she assured him.

CHAPTER 21: RUN!!

While Irma reassured Russel, a man watched them from across the room. He was a guard and he had a gun with him, his stern face filled with scars to show the kind of rough life he lived. He watched the duo with slight interest and he wondered who the boy was and why Irma seems to care about him. He made sure to keep his gaze less suspicious, he stood at a distance far from them so he couldn't hear what they talked about but he read the words through Irma's lips.

"Stay here I'll go talk to my old man, okay?"

Russel felt a little reluctant to stay behind without her with all the mean-looking men. But he mans up and nodded. Irma smiled at him and n headed up to Agalos sturdy. Seeing this the guard who had been watching them followed her, he made sure she didn't notice him behind her, and when she went Into the sturdy. He stood in front of the closed door and leaned his ear on it to eavesdrop on their conversation. Inside the sturdy Irma crossed her arms over her chest and glared at Agalos who sat across her.

He raised a brow at her, "What did I do that make you want to kill me under your gaze."

"Be honest with me old man what did you do to Russell's parents cause I know you didn't kill them" Irma inquired.

"And what makes you so sure I didn't kill them, you know what I'm capable of doing, right ?" Mr. Agalos questioned back.

Irma took a seat and sat in front of him "Yeah I know you're heartless, I also know you don't act without a reason….. You told me you wouldn't hurt Russell's parents and that's why I told you where they were, you aren't the type to lie so tell me the truth"

Irma knew her father too well, he was a man of his word and he never takes his words back. And he was a principled and disciplined man

"Hmmm why do care about Russell's parents so much" Mr.Agalos'ss lips tugged up in a proud smile.

He knew Irma would see through him.

"Well, Russel is my friend and his parents have been really nice to me so I guess I don't want harm to come to them" Irma replied unsure of her answer.

She doubted if she just saw Russel as a friend or more, but she does know that she doesn't want to see him hurt. Hearing this Mr.Agalos' eyes turned dark and his gaze became sinister.

"No, Father please don't hurt him" Irma ran after Mr. Agalos to stop him from getting to Russel.

The guard who have been eavesdropping behind the closed door hid quickly from them. He has barely heard the conversation Irma and Mr. Agalos had, but he could guess M.r Agalos would hurt or kill somebody from the little he heard.

"I will kill that stupid boy, non of the Pennington's must live, the mafia should be mine and mine alone and I will kill every one of them to make sure of that " Mr. Agalos roared.

"No father stop it" Irma threw herself at him but Mr. Agalos pushed her away and she tripped and fell.

"Guards Guards get that boy" Mr. Agalos ordered the moment he got downstairs.

Russel stood from the sofa in confusion, he wondered why Mr. Agalos was yelling when suddenly Irma yelled from behind him.

"Russel run!! Get out of here!! Run and Save your life" she yelled.

"What are you buffoons staring at, get him" Mr . Agalos yelled.

The men did just that before Russel could run away.

"Well take him to the basement and you lock up Irma in her room," Mr. Agalos ordered.

Two female guards grabbed Irma and began dragging her from the scene while she kept screaming. Russel was completely helpless in the arms of the guards who held him. His heart pounded and threatened to burst out of his chest with each beat. He was thrown on the cold basement floor the moment they got there. Mr. Agalos ordered his men to leave and then he turned to Russel with an evil smile. Russel almost pissed his pants when his cold evil gaze swept past his body. He wanted to beg for his life but the word refused to come out of his mouth.

"You know what boy I gave your parents a special gift and I'll give you the same," Agalos walked to a corner and brought out a syringe filled with blue liquid just like the one he injected Russell's parents with.

Then be walked back to Russel

"No sir I don't need your gift, please let me go" Russel forced our words.

"Don't worry boy this won't hurt too much" with that Agalos snapped Russell's neck with one slight move.

Russel fell unconscious and Agalos injected him. He placed Russell's limp body into a minecart, broke the lock on a door, and opened it, he then pushed the mine cart near the door and let it go. And the mine cart went underground just like his parents. Satisfied with that Mr. Agalos closed the door and opened a hidden compartment in the wall. He pressed in a 6-digit passcode and the door locked, no one would be able to open the door without a key and passcode. He then left the Basement.

CHAPTER 22: THEY'RE ALIVE

"Agalos have succeeded in wiping off the entire Pennington lineage and he has taken full control over the mafia...... And Irma Agalos seems to be affected by her friend's death and so she has turned rebellious to Agalos," Zord's assistant filled him with all the details their spy got...

His lips stretched into a sinister smile.

"Well well well, Agalos have made things easier for me, no obstacles from the Pennington's would stop me now... And try to her that Irma on our side, she would be of great use to us, a rebellious child would want to get back at him for what he's done, and I'll take over the mafia once she deals with him... Quick send someone to her we have no time to lose" Zord ordered.

"I'm on it sire," his assistant said and left the room.

"The Pennington couple that was found and killed by Agalos had a grown-up son but Agalos had killed him too along with his parents..... It is said that Irma has become worse after his death because they were friends before Agalos killed him....." Gaxton's assistant paused for his boss to say something.

"They aren't dead," Gaxton said as they blew past his face.

"Huh who?" His assistant asked cluelessly.

Gaxton walked to the chair and sat down taking a cup of coffee to his lips from the table of pastries in front of him. He took a sip before replying to his assistant

"Agalos didn't kill the Pennington couple and their son."

"But if he didn't kill them, then where are they and why did they suddenly disappear?" His assistant inquired.

"Agalos is a smart ass. He acts like he's the bad guy ….. He's protecting those Penningtons but no matter what, their fortune would be mine" Gaxton explained.

His assistant didn't say anything further, he doubted what his boss said but since his boss never jokes around and definitely not the Pennington Fortune.

"Get the men ready we will soon go at war with the Pennington for the fortune" with that Gaxton left the garden leaving his assistant behind.

Underground in San Antonio, In a Gold and Diamond Mine:

Russel groaned, opening his eyes. He felt pains in his neck, arms, back, and legs due to the uncomfortable position he wanted in the cart. He sat up and squinted his eyes taking in his surroundings. Glittery beautiful Diamonds and gold stuck in the mine wall. And there were carts filled with diamonds and gold. Russel gawked at them, he has never seen so many riches in his life. He got out of the cart and stretched his body, feeling the liquid Agalos injected into him, wear off. He brought out his phone from his pocket and tried to turn it on. It didn't; it appears that the phone was out of battery.

Just like Irma and Agalos had told him, he began walking down the mine admiring the beauty of the gold and diamonds as he passed. He passed a particular purple diamond and felt like taking it but he restrained himself. It didn't belong to him so he couldn't take it, after walking a distance he could hear the clanking of mine axes and the chattering of people and the sounds of minecarts moving. He walked on and came face to face with mine workers. A man in his fifties noticed him and called the attention of others.

"Hey, look it's Mr. Pennington, c'mon let's go get him," the man said and began walking toward Russel.

The man looked friendly and nice. He tipped his hat when he got to Russel.

"Welcome Amigo Mr. Agalos told us to expect your arrival please come this way," the man said and Russel nodded.

Irma had told him a man would take him to his parents when he got to the mine. The man began leading Russel away. They passed men, and women who worked in the mine, and some children were playing in the mine too. They picked pieces of gold they could find and went home with them. From the facial expressions of the workers, they enjoyed their work and chatted as they mined for gold and diamonds. The man led Russel out of the mine and they got onto a truck, the truck drove for a while before stopping in front of a beautiful giant build. It looked like a castle with the towers that surrounded it, Russel gasped taking in the beauty.

"C'mon amigo we're here" the man tapped Russel out of his reverie.

They walked past a water fountain surrounded by pretty blooming roses. They got to the huge front door of the castle and after the man talked to the guards stationed at the door they were let in. Just as they got into the living room which was like a house on its own, Russel froze on the spot. In front of him stood his parents. Larry and Sabrina are alive and healthy looking better than usual.

"MOM?...DAD?"...

CHAPTER 23: BLOODY MURDERER

"Oh, my baby" Sabrina and Russel engulfed themselves in a bone-crushing hug with Sabrina sobbing.

"My baby I'm so glad you're okay, you aren't hurt, right? Agalos didn't hurt you right?" She examined them to see if he had any wounds on him.

"No mom I'm good, but how did you get here" Russel inquired and Larry hugged him and tapped his cheeks.

"I thought we were dead, the moment Agalos injected me and I felt the pains in my body I thought that was the end and we would die..... But who knew Agalos had other plans, the liquid was just to make us unconscious through the entire trip underground... As it is, we are in San Antonio, and this is the Pennington ancestral home, my great great great great great great grandfather built it...... And we aren't a mafia family, that is just a cover-up for who we really are. Our family comes from a long generation of gold miners and it's been passed down from generation to generation...." And Larry went on to explain the real identity and history of the Penningtons and the identity of Agalos.

The Pennington was a gold miner family and they owned a huge underground mine that stretches across San Antonio and Mazatlan Mexico. In recent years the world's biggest diamond was found in their mine, it had a net worth of 100 billion dollars considering how rare and beautiful it is. It is considered Pennington's fortune and it is hidden in a place that only the

Penningtons know of. Now the Agalos families are mafias and the secret guardians of the Penningtons. Each member of the Pennington family has their personal secret guard, Mr. Agalos was Larry's elder brother's guard. But sadly, Gaxton Tarzena from a gold industry in Tijuana Mexico assassinated Larry's brother. He wanted to seize the fortune but he couldn't get it and based on the rumors surrounding the Pennington family being mafias he couldn't get any possible leads on where the fortune could be. Only one in a million people know the Penningtons as gold and diamond miners, to the outside world they are mafias but to the insiders they are miners. Agalos started the rumors and he'll keep it that way for the safety of everyone. Russel let all this information sink in then he had a flashback of the photos Irma sent him when she was talking with Mr. Agalos.

**RUSSEL FLASHBACKED:

Inside the sturdy Irma crossed her arms over her chest and glared at Agalos who sat across her. He raised a brow at her "What did I do that make you want to kill me under your gaze."

"Be honest with me old man what did you do to Russell's parents cause I know you didn't kill them" Irma inquired.

"And what makes you so sure I didn't kill them, I'm pretty heartless?" Mr. Agalos questioned back.

Irma took a seat and sat in front of him "Yeah I know you're heartless, I also know you don't act without a reason..... You told me you wouldn't hurt Russell's parents and that's why I told you where they were, you aren't the type to lie so tell me the truth."

Irma knew her father too well, he was a man of his word and he never takes his words back. And he was a principled and disciplined man.

"Hmmm why do care about Russell's parents so much" Mr. Agalos's lips tugged up in a proud smile. He knew Irma would see through him.

"Well Russel is my friend and his parents have been really nice to me so I guess I don't want harm to come to them" Irma replied unsure of her answer.

She doubted if she just saw Russel as a friend or more, but she does know that she doesn't want to see him hurt. Hearing this Mr. Agalos's eyes turned dark and his gaze became sinister. He opened a drawer and brought a slip of paper and pen, then he began writing on it.

"What are you...doing.,"

Mr. Agalos hushed her.

He then wrote on the paper and then handed it to him: "WE CAN'T TALK OUT LOUD IN THE HOUSE ABOUT RUSSEL AND HIS FAMILY, WE WILL COMMUNICATE THROUGH LETTER WRITING, THERE ARE TOO MANY SPIES IN THE HOUSE AND I DON'T WANT TO PUT THE PENNINGTONS IN DANGER... I DIDN'T KILL RUSSEL PARENTS, AS WE SPEAK THEY'RE SAFE IN SAN ANTONIO, SAFE FROM ANY POSSIBLE HARM FOR NOW....... THEY COULD BE IN DANGER IF I LEAVE THEM IN MAZATLAN, AS FOR YOUR FRIEND I WILL HAVE TO TAKE HIM AWAY FROM HERE TOO CAUSE HE'S ALSO IN GRAVE DANGER... AND I NEED YOUR HELP, WE'LL HAVE TO PUT UP AN ACT TO MAKE SURE HE GETS TO SAN ANTONIO SAFELY."

That's what is written on the paper, Irma frowned confused. She was about to ask him what he meant from what he wrote but remembered his warning from the paper.

She turned it over and began writing: "WHAT EXACTLY IS GOING ON?"

She wrote and handed it to him.

He read and then began writing on another paper.: "I WILL EXPLAIN MOST OF THE DETAILS LATER BUT FOR NOW, WE NEED TO GET YOUR FRIEND OUT OF HERE...

THERE'S A BASEMENT IN THE HOUSE THAT HAS A DOOR THAT LEADS TO AN UNDERGROUND MINE…… WE WOULD ACT AS IF I WILL ACTUALLY KILL HIM BUT I WILL MAKE HIM UNCONSCIOUS AND SEND HIM TO SAN ANTONIO THROUGH THE MINE WHERE HE WILL MEET HIS PARENTS….. WE WILL KEEP ON ACTING LIKE WE AREN'T ON GOOD TERMS FOR OVER A MONTH JUST SO NO ONE GETS SUSPICIOUS. … THEN I'LL SEND YOU TO HIM AND YOU WILL TEACH HIM MARITAL ACTS FOR HIM TO DEFEND HIMSELF AND HIS FAMILY FORTUNE…… DON'T ASK WHAT THE FORTUNE IS YOU'LL FIND OUT ABOUT THAT LATER, SO SEND A TEXT TO HIM AND TELL HIM EVERYTHING I'VE TOLD YOU AND IT'S SHOW TIME."

He handed the slip to her. She read, then smirked and nodded, then she texted Russel and that's when the acting started.

***END OF FLASHBACK.

"So you're basically saying that we're rich, like filthy rich, because that's the part I want to be sure of the most ?" Russel asked and Larry nodded.

"Yes my boy, it's all an act to protect all of us, we were hiding from the rivals and not from Agalos "

"Wow so my whole life has been a lie, a good white lie" Russel exclaimed.

"Yes baby but now you need to rest, come let me take you to your room and then I bring some snacks for you," Sabrina said and pulled Russel into an elevator that took them to the second floor.

Russel gasped as he looked around the interior. He settled into a room and slept off on the soft king-sized bed. A month lip.

Mazatlan/Mexico; Agalos residence:

It was past midnight and Irma just got home, she rode her bike into the yard and parked. Under her helmet, she put on her most angry expression before taking it off. She got off the bike and tossed the key carelessly to a guard. She sauntered into the house and found Mr. Agalos in a fit of rage in the living room. She rolled her eyes and made to walk past him when his thunderous voice stopped her in her tracks.

"Now stop right there you silly brat, what time is it?" He yelled.

"Oh please, dad you have no right to control me, as far as I know, I'm an adult and I can do whatever I please" she retorted not turning to face him.

"Oh really? you're an adult? But you live in my house and you'll do as I say," Agalos vibrates with each word.

"Haha, you want me to follow your orders? Ha, maybe I will after you bring back my Russel from the dead you bloody murderer" Irma climbed the stairs after saying that.

"Irma! Irma! Irma! Come back here this instant" Mr. Agalos yelled but a slammed door was the reply given to him.

After a few minutes, Mr. Agalos stormed up to Irma's room and barged in slamming the door behind him. He saw Irma on her bed with her phone in hand. Their gaze met and the next moment they burst into laughter.

"Haha we're good actors" Irma cackled controlling her laughs.

"Okay you remember the plan, we keep this act going till Tomorrow when you'll leave for El Paso" Agalos reminded.

"Yes I remember now go I need to sleep acting takes a whole lot of strength you know" Irma urged him out of her room.

"Okay okay, this bloody murderer will leave now" Agalos chuckled then left.

CHAPTER 24: NEW ALL

Zord Deltero Mafia:

"Irma is in the guest room, do you want to see her now" Zord's assistant informed.

Zord walked past him and out of the sturdy to the guest room meant for kidnapped victims. A guard positioned at the door of the room opened the door and paved the way for him to go In. Inside the vintage-designed room, Irma lay on the huge bed looking like a damsel in distress but she was far from a damsel in distress. She squinted her eyes to check out where she was.

"You might want to stop your acting, we got something to discuss" Zord sat on the chair placed at the foot of the bed and gazed straight at Irma's face.

She sat up and glared at Zord.

"What's the meaning of this madness Zord, I do hope you realize you have the wrong person" Irma snapped.

"The rumors are true, you are one feisty tiger aren't you?" Zord ignored her rudeness.

Without waiting for her to retort, he continued "so I heard Agalos recently assassinated your darling friend right in front of your eyes."

"So what's it to you?" Irma remarked her expression softening.

Seeing this, Zord stood up and began pacing around the room.

"Poor boy, he must have begged for mercy from Agalos, but knowing Agalos he killed him anyway despite the fact he was your friend"

"Why are you telling me stuff I already know?" Irma's voice cracked lightly

Zord sighed pathetically and stood by the foot of the bed returning his gaze to Irma's

"I can imagine how bad it must be to have such a heartless father and the hate you feel for him is exactly what you should feel towards him….. Agalos has always been heartless and a cold-blooded person even to his family, it boils me to see such things."

"Don't act like you're any different from him, you're just the same bloody killers " Irma yelled

"Yeah you're right I am a bloody killer, but I'm gonna make you an exception, I'll help you take revenge on Agalos for what he did to you….. Join me and we will defeat Agalos together and you'll make him pay for taking your friend away from you…… Let's join hands Irma and bring Agalos down" Zord preached.

"Tsk tsk I should've known you didn't have anything reasonable to say, seriously you expect me to go against my father? Oh please, that is a fat chance I can never do that" Irma refused Zord's offer.

Zord smiled like he expected her to say that.

"I do appreciate and admire the respect you have for Agalos but he doesn't deserve it…… Get your revenge on him, kill him and take up his mafia and everybody wins that way" Zord persuaded.

Irma bows her head appearing to consider Zord's idea.

"So will we be allies?" Zord asked expectantly.

"Just one question, why do you insist on me getting revenge and why do you want me to be allied with you?" Irma inquired with her eyebrows furrowed as she stared at him questioningly.

"Good questions, from the beef you have with your father I can see you want revenge but you don't know how to… And for the ally part, I just want to help bring Agalos down to rock bottom " Zord replied.

Irma scrutinized Zord before nodding a no and refusing his help to get revenge.

"Okay you can leave now but whenever you change your mind you can always come to find me," Zord said then he ordered a guard to drive Irma back to the airport.

The car was stopped by a roadside and Irma got out of the car after hesitating for a while.

She turned to the guard and asked: "Do you mind driving me back to Zord I forgot something."

Without waiting for his reply Irma entered the car again and he drove her back to Zord's estate. She was brought in to meet Zord. This time he lay on a bed and took skinny girls who were giving him a massage.

"I change my mind I will be your ally I want revenge from Agalos for what he did to Russel "Irma's dead parents.

"Excellent I knew you would be too smart to pass up an opportunity " Zord opened an eye to stare at her.

"So what is the plan" Irma inquired.

"For this plan, you designed for its successfulness, I suggest I make less communication contact with you to avoid suspicion from that sick old man," Irma told Zord in one of their discussions.

Now she had the plans of Zord, she needed to fulfill the second part of her assignment…

and that is to train Russel in martial acts because he and his fortune had a terrible hurricane of trouble coming at than with a high velocity.

"There's no need for you to be careful I've got everything under control" Zord grunted brushing off her suggestion.

���������������� ������� ������"

Instead of saying that Irma said "I know better than to leave the entire plans in your hands, for all I know you could only be using me"

'�������   ���������
��������������   ������'����
������� �� ������� ���� ����
���������������'

"Fine, you can leave the premises and go wherever you like, only make sure to keep in touch and alert us of your every move....."

Irma cut Zord, "So what now? I'm a criminal because I choose to take your help. Listen, old man, you take orders from me and not the other way round……. And if you don't like that then I might as well walk out of this deal."

Zord's eyes narrowed and a frown crept up his face but it disappeared within a second.

"Oh yes we'll take orders from you, after all, you have more power than me in the mafia world, my apologies…..����ñ����������" Zord kissed his teeth in annoyance but he did make sure to keep that annoyance out of his tone.

"Flattery doesn't charge this battery, now we proceed with the plan in a month from now… Till then we'll go on with our normal lives like we never met……got it" Irma kept her tone firm and unwavering and gazed straight into the short fat man's eyes.

Irma stood at 6 feet tall while Zord was only 5.2 feet tall so he had to raise his neck to stare directly at Irma's face.

"Yeah loud and clear " he muttered internally grumbling.

He wanted to get the plan done within a week or two but now his lady '�������' pushed the date to four weeks.

"Good I'll see you then" Irma walked out of the room with an air of arrogance.

She exited the building and hailed a cab to a location.

Inside Zord's residence, he was boiling with rage. He wanted to be the boss of his master plan and order her around but she turned it around now he is the one who gets bossed.

"Follow her and keep track of her dealings" Zord ordered a guard.

Junkyard:

Irma walked into a steely, smelly, deserted junkyard filled with rubbish covering her nose with a perfumed hanky. Disgusted with the running rodents and howling of stray dogs she hurried through the debris of junk and motor parts for a container. With her cellphone touch, she looked around for it, finally coming across a greasy old ordinarily looking container Irma sighed. She broke the hinge holding the door of the container with an iron rod, moved the container door from it, and went in. A long rectangular box package awaited her, she tore open the package and uncovered its content revealing a human prototype mega robot. A custom-made human prototype robot that was a photocopy of Irma. The robot was made and programmed to be Irma and so with a push of a button on the neck of robot Irma, she came alive and stood from the box. Human Irma smirked.

Gaxton Tarzena mafia:

"There aren't any new updates on the fortune of the Penningtons" Gaxton's assistant said.

"Isn't that Russel making any plans on making their fortune public" Gaxton inquired frowning.

"Apparently nothing, seems like he getting used to the luxury he has now," his assistant said.

"We'll have to delay our attack till when they go public, the boy will probably be immature and make a dumb move that would give us an advantage over him."

"You sure about that boss, Irma and Agalos probably have a trick up their sleeves"

"They won't get between my plans not anymore," Gaxton said dismissively.

CHAPTER 25: IRMA SAVES THE DAY

"Okay so you stay back here in El Paso and take my place, who things are moving too fast but anyway we'll get through this... now you have my memory data and you look exactly like me, you can leave now" Human Irma talked to Robot Irma.

Robot Irma walked out of the container like a normal human being then she left the junkyard with Zord's guard following her. Human Irma applied makeup and changed her appearance from a young lady to an old saggy woman. She held a crutch and left the junkyard and hailed a cab to a terminal. She boarded a train like an old lady and traveled to San Antonio. She got to San Antonio in the dead of night and took a cab to P.G.E.

Pennington Gold Estate:

The taxi arrived not too long later in front of the Estate Gates, she paid the driver and got out of the car. Holding the crutch and bending, she bypassed the guard who stood in front of the gates and walked to a retina scan machine. Her eye was scanned and the electronic gate opened. Under the glares of the guards, she entered the estate, and the gates shut behind her. Finally, after all these months, she'll see Russel, that thought alone gave her bubbles and immense joy.

Three weeks later:

"Ahh, Russel you're too fast, hey watch out... Gosh, I'm not an enemy, don't hit me like that, ah...... You ungrateful jerk ah" Irma screamed as Russel chased her.

The martial arts had taken a big turn on Irma and she's now the victim. Russel sometimes gets caught up in the training and sometimes beats her up, not too hard though. Just a swollen forehead or twisted knee, he felt bad for it but he couldn't stop himself. He became brave, stronger, and fiercer thanks to Irma's training, which Irma is regretting cause she has become a mannequin to Russel. He caught up with her and tripped her off her feet, she fell backward and hit the ground with a thud.

Russel stood over her with a sinister grin.

"Okay alright you win please give me a break, I still got a rib to care for" she pleaded.

Russel grunted and pulled her roughly from the ground, she hit her head on his chest due to the force he used.

"Get well soon," Russel said his voice deep and hoarse and his breath fanning on her face.

She gulped at how close they were to each other's bodies. A blush crept to her cheeks and she pushed him away. Russel smirked and left her On the training grounds. Irma watched his now broad back disappear into the house, she heaved a sigh to calm herself before sauntering into the house. Russel was nowhere in sight when she got in.

"Hey where's Russel, " she asked a guard passing by.

"Young sir is in his room with a lady ma'am" the guard replied and continued on his way.

A frown made its way to her face as she remembered Russel Casanova's ways. Not a day or two passes without a lady coming to the house to visit Russel, Russel takes the lady to his room and they do kinds of stuff and whatnot. And then the lady leaves with a flushed face and ruffled hair giving the impression that something immoral happened in Russell's room. The new Russel wasn't the same as the old nerdy one and Irma hates it but what can she do than to nurse her breaking heart? Having a one-sided love.

A week later:

World's Biggest Diamond On Its Way To Go Public. This Huge Diamond Is Sailing On A Grand Ship, Special Armed Forces Guard It On Its Trip To Europe. The Pennington Fortune has gone public and the world is in chaos. Gangs and mobs are planning to Heist billions worth of diamonds. Gaxton isn't sitting still, he and his men plan to raid the ship. And Zord too is about to take action on Agalos Mafia.

A war is awaiting...

Pennington Mansion, Irma's Room:

Irma pulled up black shiny, silky cargo pants up her smooth legs and her waist. She zipped it up and tucked in her black tank top, she tightened a pistol hostel around her waist and leg and shoved pistols in them. Her gun pocket held an Ak 47, loads of bullets, grenades, pocket knives, and other weapons as well as other devices. She slid her feet into a pair of black ankle boots, tied her hair into a ponytail, and used a black bandana to keep it in place. She applied black lipstick and mascara and wore a pair of earrings, wore gloves, and a mask over her nose and mouth. She threw the gun pocket over her shoulder and left the room after checking her outfit.

She walked to Russell's room in the mansion and knocked on his door. She opened the door and went in without waiting for a '������ ����'. A guy sat on a couch in Russell's room and he had a box in front of him. Russel stood in front of a ceiling-to-floor mirror adjusting the black tailored suit he wore. The suit fitted his broad back and shoulders perfectly, definitely not an eyesore.

Russel saw her through the mirror and said "You really should learn how to knock and wait before entering someone's room."

Irma rolled her eyes staring questioningly at the dude who sat in Russell's room.

Russel turned from the mirror and said to the guy "you can leave I'll see you later for the designs"

"Sure thing hottie, mmh" the guy blew a kiss at Russel before exiting the room with his box of jewelry.

"Who was that gay ?" Irma inquired.

"You don't need to know, let's head off" Russel walked past her out of the room.

Irma frowned and followed behind him scowling and cursing at him, 'Dumb head if it wasn't for me you'd still be a chicken. Because you've got some sexy ass you became a casanova and possibly gay. What else would you be doing in your room with a guy and he even blew you a kiss before he left? I can't believe you've become a jerk, punk. Proud chicken head, you've become disrespectful towards me, you should be thankful I'm your secret guardian and that I like you, else you'd be dead meat,' Irma was so lost in thoughts cursing Russel that she didn't notice when he stopped walking and she bumped head first onto his back.

He turned to face her "Are you a pig"

Irma blinked her eyes dumbly.

"You better stop grunting or I'll be convinced you're a pig" with that said Russel continued on his way with a smile teasing his lips.

Irma's expression turned grim and she screamed inwardly hurling all sorts of incoherent insults at Russel. She huffed under her mask and went downstairs, Russel was there with his parents and a few guards.

"Hurry up we're getting late, we shouldn't leave our enemies waiting" Russel stuffed his hands into his suit pants pockets and walked through the front doors.

His parents followed behind him with some guards. Russel and his parents entered a white limo with silver trim, two black jeeps escorted the limo as they drove out of the estate. A brand new power bike was brought to Irma, she got on it and turned it on... She drove out of the estate taking a detour to the city's jetty. She got her power bike on a private yacht, the yacht was rented to host a party. The yacht soon departed from the harbor and got on the sea. A few hours after the yacht departed from the harbor, a ship was set to sail. At the harbor reporters surrounded the area trying to get a glimpse of the ship and the world's biggest diamond that was showcased in a glass. The sun reflected on the diamonds giving off rays of light.

Russel stood in front of the diamond glass and answered a few questions thrown at him by reporters.

"Sir, what can you tell us about the diamond?"

"Is this diamond going public? Yes, yes it is going public in Europe" Russel answered smartly.

"So you're just going to sell it off"

"It will be exhibited at an auction..."Russel replied.

A reporter interjected, "Why don't you keep it as a trademark of your family?"

"Who are you, Pennington's mafias or Miners?" questions popped from the crowd of reporters and they pushed themselves forward to get more information.

Luckily Russell's guards surrounded him and helped him onto the ship with the diamond. The ship set sail and began drifting from the harbor.

Gaxton Deltero:

Gaxton was helped Into a submarine along with his assistant and two guards. A submarine sailor drove the submarine underwater. More of the Gaxton guards followed underwater with diving suits. They moved fast and soon caught up with the sailing ship where Russe was. Russel was in the control room with some guards. They watched Gaxton's submarine approach the ship from the ship's underwater CCTV

"Let's make things easy for them, shall we?" Russel pushed a button and the ship's underwater platform unlocked.

A guard from Gaxton's side checked the platform and pulled it open. Gaxton chuckled at how easily they were able to gain access to the ship.

Gaxton was given an oxygen mask, he wore it and swam out of the submarine and into the ship's platform.

His assistant followed with his numerous guards

They treated the last deck carefully, shooting any guards of Russel they came in contact with.

They soon got to the second deck where Russel and his parents were having a meal. Gaxton guards shot Russel guards before the guard could react, startling the family.

"Oh sorry did I startle you? haha," Gaxton laughed.

Russel stood from the dining and faced Gaxton, "Who are you and how did you get in here?"

"I'm your worst nightmare and your foolishness gave me access to your ship" Gaxton replied.

"So what's your business here? Why are my men getting shot?" Russel asked his expression calm which annoyed Gaxton.

He expected Russel to shiver in fear or panic like a normal teenage boy.

"We have no problem with you boy just stay put and we'll be on our way" Gaxton gestured to his guards to surround and search the ship for the diamond.

"Hey what do you think you're. ...hey" a guard snuck up on Russel and held his hands down.

Two other guards held Larry and Sabrina.

Gaxton smiled and sat on a chair crossing his legs.

"Ahh, the luxury of the Penningtons, oh how much I crave for it…..

I would've gotten it sooner if it wasn't for Agalos and his smart tricks but now it's my time" Gaxton ran his palm on the goat leather couch.

"I suggest you don't struggle boy, you are at a disadvantage if you choose to fight back….. Tell us where the diamond is on the ship and we'll get it and be out of here."

"Over my dead body would I let an old shit bag get his disgusting hands on that diamond" Russel cussed.

Gaxton frowned, his eyes darkened but a smile broke out on his face. A guard passed him a gun and he pointed it at Sabrina.

"The diamond boy or your mom gets it" Gaxton cocked the gun.

"What don't you dare hurt my mom" Russel struggled to get the guards off him.

Gaxton snickered and fired the gun at Sabrina the bullet pierced into her chest and she fell to the ground with a thud and her eyes closed with blood sipping out her chest.

"Mom!"

"Sabrina!"

Russel and larry called.

"Next will be your father boy, the diamond " Gaxton demanded.

Russel glared at Gaxton and said: "Room 08."

"Great, you chose well boy"

A few guards went to the room number mentioned by Russel and retrieved the glass box containing the diamond.

Gaxton's eyes showed on seeing it.

"Ahh I guess we're done here………oh wait we aren't" Gaxton pointed his gun at Larry and pulled the trigger.

It hit Larry in the chest

"No! You said you just wanted the diamond and now you have it, why did you shoot him" Russel growled.

"Oh did I say that ?" Gaxton feigned being clueless. "Oh, well, maybe I changed my mind" He shrugged.

"You'll never get away with this " Russel threatened.

"Well boys, it looks like I already have……"

Several loud groaning voices cut off Gaxton. His guards were getting attacked by an invisible source. One by one his guards were getting beaten, Russel, seeing Gaxton was distracted freed himself from the guards holding him and knocked them out. His guards who were supposedly dead after they were shot by Gaxton's men stood up from the floor and grabbed Gaxton.

"Wha..what…what's happening?" Gaxton was frightened at the swift change of events.

Larry and Sabrina also stood up with smiles on their faces. The invincible source became visible and turned out to be Irma in an invisible camouflage costume.

"I'm right on time" she landed a kick on a guard's private part and his eyes bulge out as he screamed in pain.

"Yup you sure are, are you surprised Gaxton?" Russel turned to Gaxton with a mocking stare.

"How did you do that, you two parents you supposed to be dead" Gaxton pointed at Larry and Sabrina.

The duo smiled at themselves then removed a bulletproof vest from under their clothes, they threw it at Gaxton's face. Russel's guards, parents, and himself all wore bulletproof vests to protect themselves. Seeing his boss getting captured, Gaxton's assistant grabbed the diamond box and ran off. He ran to the last deck and got on a jet ski, he found the key and turned it on, and drove out of the ship's platform.

"Ooh seems like your trusted man just abandoned you "Russel snickered

Gaxton roared in anger.

His perfect plan had just been ruined.

"Um, Russel shouldn't we chase after the diamond " Irma inquired.

"Nope, we shouldn't chase a fake" Russel replied.

Just as he said that the diamond box began beeping loudly and it exploded. Turns out the diamond and its box the Gaxton assistant ran with was a bomb.

"You tricked me, boy, you tricked me, you'll pay for this" Gaxton struggled out of the guard's hold and pointed his gun at Russel, he pulled the trigger immediately. Seeing this Irma ran in front of Russel and covered him with her body, the bullet hit her back and she winced as the bullet pierced into her back.

"Irma!" Russel panicked taking her into his arms.

"I'm fine…..it doesn't hurt…….focus on Gaxton" Irma struggled to talk as she began losing consciousness.

"Don't let him get away guys!….. mom quick call paramedics, Irma please keep your eyes open don't close 'em."

CHAPTER 26: FINALE OF BOOK 1

Zord Deltero:

Zord's plan to acquire the Agalos mafia failed, thanks to Irma that ruined his plans and made hitches. Zord was arrested and sentenced to 5 years imprisonment for trespassing and attempted.

Mr. Agalos:

Since he had no heir to take over the mafia from him, Agalos handed his mafia to his most trusted guard, seems Irma wasn't up to continue living the mafia life. Now, Agalos lives like a normal man and probably finds his own love.

Larry and Sabrina:

They continued being good parents and had a smooth marriage without any hiccups as usual.

Meliana, Tania, and Nickko:

Meliana continued in her old sassy ways but she did become focused on her studies and manage to get a high share in her father's company.

Tania and Nickko got into a rough relationship, Nickko's bisexuality brought numerous arguments and fights, but neither of them broke off the relationship.

Gaxton Tarzena:

Handed to the police and sentenced to life imprisonment without parole. He had a rough time in jail with his fellow inmates and got beaten up a few times.

Irma and Russel:

Well, guess we'll find out what happened with those two in Book 2 of "The Mafia Identity."

The End Of "The Mafia Identity" 1…

The Mafia Identity 2

coming in January.